Kneading the Truth

The Sourdough Sleuth Mysteries, Volume 1

Gracelynne MacAllister

Published by Gracelynne MacAllister, 2024.

Kneading the Truth
Book 1 of *The Sourdough Sleuth Mysteries*
Copyright © 2024 by Gracelynne MacAllister
No part of this book may be reproduced, distributed, or transmitted in any form or by any means, including photocopying, recording, or other electronic or mechanical methods, without the prior written permission of the publisher, except in the case of brief quotations embodied in critical reviews and certain other noncommercial uses permitted by copyright law. For permission requests, write to the publisher, addressed "Attention: Permissions Coordinator," at the address below.

Gracelynne MacAllister

Book Group: https://www.facebook.com/groups/1393323041237972/

Seed/Garden/Canning/Lifestyle Group: https://www.facebook.com/groups/395868519945652/

This is a work of fiction. Names, characters, businesses, places, events, and incidents are either the product of the author's imagination or used in a fictitious manner. Any resemblance to actual persons, living or dead, or actual events is purely coincidental.

Cover Design by: Canva
First Edition: September 2024
For more information, visit: https://rusticroots.blog/

Coming Soon from Gracelynne MacAllister:
October 2024: Pumpkin Spice and Everything Nice
November 2024: A Harvest of Love
December 2024: Evergreen Wishes

Chapter 1: The Yeast of Time

The early morning light filtered through the windows of "The Yeast of Time," casting a warm glow over the rustic wooden countertops and the assortment of baking tools neatly arranged in their places. The bakery was still quiet, the air filled with the comforting scent of yeast and flour mingling with a hint of cinnamon. Harper MacLeod stood at the center of her domain; her hands deep in a bowl of dough that was slowly coming to life under her practiced touch.

The rhythm of kneading was second nature to her by now, each push and pull of the dough a meditative act. It was in these quiet, solitary moments that Harper felt most connected to her ancestors, imagining them doing the same, centuries ago, in kitchens that were perhaps not so different from her own. Her grandmother, Fiona, often spoke of those ancestors with a kind of reverence, weaving tales of their life in the Scottish Highlands, where bread was not just food but a symbol of survival and tradition.

Harper's bakery was more than just a business; it was a legacy. The heart of "The Yeast of Time" was a 400-year-old sourdough starter, passed down through generations of MacLeods. Fiona had entrusted her with the starter, along with the family recipes and the stories that went with them. The starter was a living link to their ancestors in Scotland, and Harper treated it with the reverence it deserved. It was a responsibility she didn't take lightly—this bubbling, tangy mixture that had fed her family for centuries, now sat in a glass jar on the counter, alive and thriving under her care.

As she worked, Harper's thoughts drifted to her grandmother. Fiona MacLeod was a formidable woman, as strong and resilient as the Scottish mountains where she was born. Even now, in her late seventies, Fiona's mind was as sharp as ever, her stories as vivid and enthralling as they had been when Harper was a child. It was Fiona who had taught Harper the art of baking, the science behind the yeast, and the magic that happened when flour, water, and salt came together in just the right way.

Harper glanced out the window at the sleepy town of Clover Grove, where life moved at a pace that suited her just fine. The town was small, with its population just shy of 3,000, but it was full of character. The streets were lined with quaint shops, each with its own history, and the people were as much a part of the town as the buildings themselves. Harper had moved here five years ago, after a career in criminal psychology had left her longing for something simpler, something that felt real. The bakery had given her that and more—a sense of purpose and a place where she truly belonged.

She thought back to the decision that had brought her to Clover Grove. Leaving behind the city, with its relentless pace and constant noise, had been both the hardest and easiest choice of her life. In the city, Harper had been good at her job—great, even—but she had never felt at home there. The cases she worked on, the people she dealt with, the endless cycle of crime and punishment—it had worn her down, eroded something inside her that she hadn't realized was fragile until it was nearly gone.

Clover Grove had been her salvation. The small town had welcomed her with open arms, its people kind and curious but respectful of her privacy. She had found solace in the routine of baking, in the simple pleasures of kneading dough and watching it rise, of feeding the sourdough starter and knowing that she was part of a tradition that spanned centuries. Here, in this little bakery, she had found the peace that had eluded her for so long.

The bell above the door chimed softly, pulling Harper from her thoughts. She looked up to see Evelyn Hargrove, the town's librarian, stepping inside. Evelyn was in her late fifties, with graying hair pulled back into a neat bun and eyes that sparkled with a love for books and gossip alike. She was a regular at the bakery, often coming in for a scone and a chat before heading off to the library.

"Good morning, Harper," Evelyn said, her voice as warm as the freshly baked bread cooling on the racks behind the counter.

"Morning, Evelyn," Harper replied, smiling as she wiped her hands on her apron. "The usual?"

Evelyn nodded, her eyes drifting to the display case filled with scones, muffins, and loaves of sourdough. "Yes, please. And a cup of your special blend coffee, if you've got some ready."

"Coming right up," Harper said, moving to fill the order. As she prepared Evelyn's scone, she couldn't help but notice the librarian's thoughtful expression. "You seem deep in thought today. Everything alright?"

Evelyn sighed, taking a seat at one of the small wooden tables by the window. "It's just the town, you know? So much going on lately. You'd think a place like Clover Grove would be immune to big-city problems, but it seems like trouble finds its way here all the same."

Harper's curiosity piqued. "What kind of trouble?"

"Well, it's nothing too serious," Evelyn said, though her tone suggested otherwise. "But I heard from Marge over at the diner that Chef Anthony has been acting strange lately. Keeping to himself more than usual, and not as friendly as he used to be. You know how everyone loves him—always so full of life and generous with his recipes. But lately... I don't know, something just seems off."

Harper frowned as she handed Evelyn her scone and coffee. "That's odd. I haven't seen him much lately, but I always figured he was just busy with the restaurant."

"That's what I thought too," Evelyn said, taking a sip of her coffee. "But Marge swears something's wrong. She's known him for years, and she's worried."

"I'll have to check in on him," Harper said, her mind already turning over the possibilities. She had known Chef Anthony since she moved to Clover Grove. He had been one of the first to welcome her to the town, offering her tips on sourcing local ingredients and sharing stories of his culinary adventures. The idea of something being wrong with him didn't sit well with her.

"Maybe it's nothing," Evelyn said, shrugging. "But you know how it is in a small town—everyone notices when something's out of the ordinary."

Harper nodded, her thoughts lingering on Chef Anthony. "I'll see what I can find out."

Evelyn smiled, though her eyes still held that flicker of concern. "You're a good friend, Harper. I'm sure it's just a rough patch. But still, it's nice to know someone's looking out for him."

As Evelyn finished her scone and prepared to leave, Harper returned to her work, but her mind wasn't on the dough in front of her. Instead, she found herself thinking about the people of Clover Grove and how, despite its small size, the town held as many secrets as any big city.

The streets outside the bakery began to come to life as the morning progressed. Shop owners unlocked their doors, and the first wave of customers filtered into the various stores. Harper could see Mrs. Thompson, the florist, arranging a fresh delivery of flowers in her shop window, her hands moving with the precision of years spent cultivating beauty from the earth. Across the street, Mr. Jacobson was opening up the hardware store, his stooped figure moving slowly but with the same determination that had kept his business running for decades.

It was scenes like these that made Harper love Clover Grove. There was a sense of continuity here, a feeling that life moved in cycles, predictable and reassuring. But beneath that surface calm, Harper knew there were undercurrents of change, of secrets waiting to be uncovered. In her previous life as a criminal psychologist, she had learned to read people, to see beyond their words and actions to the truths they tried to hide. And lately, she had been getting the sense that Clover Grove was hiding something.

Harper finished kneading the dough and set it aside to rise, covering the bowl with a cloth. She wiped her hands on her apron again, her thoughts returning to Chef Anthony. She remembered the last time they had spoken, a brief conversation outside his restaurant. He had seemed distracted, his usual warmth tempered by a kind of preoccupation that Harper hadn't understood at the time. Now, she wondered if there had been more to it—if something had been weighing on him, something he hadn't been able to talk about.

The thought nagged at her as she continued with her morning routine. The bakery began to fill with the scent of baking bread, rich and comforting, but the comfort it usually brought was absent today. Harper's mind kept drifting back to Chef Anthony, to the worry in Evelyn's voice, to the subtle changes she had noticed in the town over the past few weeks.

As the first customers of the day began to arrive, Harper pushed her concerns to the back of her mind, focusing on the task at hand. She greeted each customer with a smile, chatting with them about the weather, their families, and the usual small-town gossip. But even as she did, she couldn't shake the feeling that something was brewing in Clover Grove—something that was about to come to a head.

When the morning rush finally subsided, Harper took a moment to catch her breath. She poured herself a cup of coffee and sat down at one of the tables, gazing out the window at the bustling street. The sun was fully up now, casting long shadows across the pavement, and the town was alive with activity.

But Harper's thoughts were far from the peaceful scene outside. She had a sinking feeling that the calm was deceptive, that there was a storm on the horizon. And as she sat there, sipping her coffee, she couldn't help but wonder what role she would play in the events that were about to unfold.

The bell above the door chimed again, and Harper looked up to see another customer entering. She set her coffee aside and rose to greet them, her thoughts still heavy with the weight of the unknown. But as she moved back behind the counter, she made a silent promise to herself: whatever was coming, she would be ready.

For now, though, she would focus on what she did best—baking. And if the past had taught her anything, it was that even in the midst of uncertainty, there was comfort to be found in the simple, steady rhythm of kneading dough and the promise of warm, fresh bread.

Chapter 2: Whispers in the Wind

The day passed in a blur of baking and serving customers, but Harper couldn't shake the uneasy feeling that had settled over her since her conversation with Evelyn. Each transaction, each smile she gave to her regulars felt mechanical, as if she were going through the motions while her mind wandered elsewhere. By the time the last customer had left and the bakery was closed for the night, the feeling had only intensified, gnawing at her with a persistence she couldn't ignore.

She decided to take a walk, hoping the cool evening air would clear her head. The night had always been Harper's solace, a time when she could unwind and let her thoughts flow freely. The streets of Clover Grove were quiet at this hour, bathed in the soft glow of streetlamps that cast long shadows on the pavement. The town, so full of life during the day, now seemed almost otherworldly, as if it held secrets that only revealed themselves when the sun went down.

As she walked, Harper thought about Chef Anthony and the strange behavior Evelyn had mentioned. The more she mulled it over, the more the pieces didn't fit. Chef Anthony was a man of routine, a fixture in the community whose presence brought comfort to those around him. He was known for his generosity and warmth, always ready with a smile or a piece of advice, especially when it came to food. If something was troubling him, it must have been serious. And if he was acting out of character, it meant whatever was bothering him had been festering for some time.

KNEADING THE TRUTH

Harper paused in front of the town square, her eyes drawn to the old clock tower that stood sentinel over the town. The clock's hands moved with a steady, reassuring rhythm, but tonight, even that seemed out of sync with the world around her. She wrapped her arms around herself, not so much from the chill in the air, but from the growing sense of unease that had settled in her chest.

She was about to turn back toward the bakery when she noticed a figure standing outside Chef Anthony's restaurant, *Le Petit Boulanger*. The restaurant was a charming little place, with its warm yellow walls and hand-painted sign that featured a loaf of bread and a rolling pin. But tonight, it looked different—more like a haunted house than the cozy, inviting space it usually was.

The figure standing by the door was tall and broad-shouldered, his stance tense as he stared at the darkened windows. Harper hesitated, her steps slowing as she took in the scene. Something about the way he stood, so still and focused, sent a shiver down her spine. She almost turned back, but curiosity got the better of her. After all, this was Clover Grove—what harm could there be in saying hello?

As she drew closer, the figure turned slightly, and Harper recognized him. Detective Ethan Callahan, the town's newest police officer, was someone she had seen around town but hadn't had many interactions with. He was still somewhat of an enigma to the people of Clover Grove—arriving from Chicago just over a year ago, he had brought with him a calm, steady demeanor that contrasted sharply with the easygoing nature of the town. He was respected, sure, but he wasn't quite one of them yet.

"Detective Callahan?" Harper called out softly as she approached. The detective turned fully to face her, and even in the dim light, Harper could see the troubled expression on his face. His usually sharp blue eyes were clouded with something she couldn't quite place—worry, perhaps, or frustration.

"Harper," he said, his voice low and rough, as if he had been lost in thought for a long time. "What are you doing out here?"

"I was just taking a walk," Harper replied, coming to stand beside him. She glanced at the restaurant's darkened windows, a cold knot forming in her stomach. "Is everything alright?"

Ethan sighed, rubbing the back of his neck as he glanced back at the restaurant. "I'm not sure. I got a call earlier—someone reported seeing Chef Anthony acting strangely near the docks late last night. When I tried to reach him today, there was no answer."

Harper's unease deepened. The docks were on the outskirts of town, a place usually reserved for fishermen and the occasional tourist. It wasn't the kind of place one went to alone, especially not in the dead of night. "Do you think something's happened to him?"

"I don't know," Ethan admitted, his voice tinged with frustration. "But I'm worried. He's not the type to just disappear without a word."

Harper looked up at the restaurant, her heart sinking. The windows were dark, the door locked tight, but there was an unsettling stillness in the air, as if the building itself was holding its breath. She could feel it, too—a sense that something was out of place, that the familiar had been touched by something unknown and unwelcome.

"Have you checked inside?" she asked, her voice barely above a whisper.

Ethan shook his head, his jaw tight. "Not yet. I don't have a warrant, and there's no sign of forced entry. But something doesn't feel right."

Harper bit her lip, her mind racing. "What if we called him? Maybe he's just out of town or something."

"I've tried," Ethan said, his frustration evident. "No answer. And no one's seen him since yesterday."

The silence between them stretched, filled with unspoken fears. Harper's concern grew, but she knew there was little she could do at the moment. "If there's anything I can do to help, let me know," she said, her voice soft, though she felt the weight of her own helplessness.

Ethan looked at her, his eyes filled with gratitude. There was something more in his gaze, something that spoke of a shared burden, a silent understanding that they were both grasping at shadows in the dark. "Thanks, Harper. I'll keep you updated."

As she walked back to the bakery, Harper couldn't shake the feeling that something terrible had happened. The night was too quiet, the town too still, and in the back of her mind, a nagging voice told her that the secrets of Clover Grove were about to be brought into the light—whether they were ready or not.

But as she walked, her thoughts kept circling back to Ethan. He had been in Clover Grove for over a year, but he remained something of a mystery to her. His arrival had been low-key, almost as if he had wanted to blend into the town without drawing too much attention. And yet, there was an intensity to him, a sense of purpose that set him apart from the laid-back pace of the town. Harper had heard snippets of his life before Clover Grove—whispers of a high-profile case in Chicago that had ended badly, of a transfer that had seemed more like an escape. But the details were vague, and Ethan wasn't one to share much about himself.

As she made her way back to the bakery, Harper found herself wondering about the man behind the badge. What had brought him to Clover Grove? And what was it about Chef Anthony's disappearance that had rattled him so much? Was it just the case, or was there something more?

The bakery was dark and quiet when Harper returned, the scents of the day's work lingering in the air. She locked the door behind her and made her way to the small apartment above the bakery where she lived. It was a cozy space, filled with the warmth of wooden furniture and soft fabrics, but tonight it felt more like a refuge, a place to retreat from the questions and doubts that had taken root in her mind.

She changed into her pajamas and made herself a cup of herbal tea, hoping it would help her unwind. But even as she sipped the warm liquid, her thoughts remained tangled, circling back to the same questions over and over again. What had happened to Chef Anthony? And why did she have the sinking feeling that this was just the beginning?

Harper set her mug down on the coffee table and leaned back on the couch, closing her eyes. She tried to focus on the comforting sounds of the night—the distant chirping of crickets, the rustling of leaves in the breeze—but her mind refused to quiet. Images flashed through her thoughts: Chef Anthony's kind smile, his eyes twinkling with mischief as he shared a secret recipe; the darkened windows of *Le Petit Boulanger*, silent and foreboding; and Ethan's troubled expression, his voice low and rough as he spoke of his worries.

She opened her eyes and stared at the ceiling, frustration gnawing at her. She wasn't used to feeling so helpless, so out of control. In her previous life, she had been the one to find the answers, to piece together the puzzle. But here, in Clover Grove, she was just a baker—a keeper of old traditions, a maker of bread and pastries. What could she do to help a man like Ethan, who was trained to deal with the unknown, to confront the darkness head-on?

But even as the doubts crept in, another part of her—the part that had once thrived on challenges, on solving the unsolvable—refused to be silenced. She might not be a detective, but she was still Harper MacLeod, and she had never been one to sit idly by while others were in need. If there was something she could do to help, she would find it. And if there were answers to be found, she would uncover them—no matter how deep they were buried.

The next morning, Harper woke early, the remnants of restless sleep clinging to her like a heavy fog. She had tossed and turned all night, her dreams filled with shadowy figures and half-heard whispers, but she couldn't remember any of it clearly. All she knew was that the uneasy feeling from the night before hadn't dissipated; if anything, it had intensified.

She got dressed and headed downstairs to the bakery, determined to lose herself in the comforting routine of baking. The process of kneading dough, of measuring out ingredients and watching them come together to create something greater, had always been a source of solace for her. Today, she needed that solace more than ever.

As the morning progressed, the bakery began to fill with the usual stream of customers. Harper greeted them with a smile, chatting with them about their lives, their families, and the latest town gossip. But even as she engaged with them, her thoughts were elsewhere, focused on the unanswered questions that hung over her like a cloud.

By the time the morning rush had subsided, Harper was exhausted, both physically and mentally. She took a moment to catch her breath, leaning against the counter as she wiped her hands on a towel. The bakery was quiet now, the scent of fresh bread lingering in the air, but the peace it usually brought her was elusive.

She was about to head to the back to start on a new batch of dough when the bell above the door jingled, signaling the arrival of a customer. Harper looked up, surprised to see Detective Ethan Callahan standing in the doorway.

"Ethan," she greeted, her voice tinged with surprise. "I didn't expect to see you here."

Ethan offered her a small smile, though it didn't reach his eyes. "Morning, Harper. I hope I'm not interrupting."

"Not at all," Harper replied, gesturing for him to come in. "I was just about to take a break. Can I get you anything?"

Ethan shook his head, his expression serious. "No, thanks. I just came by to check in and see how you're doing."

Harper studied him for a moment, noting the tension in his posture, the way his eyes seemed to flicker with a thousand unspoken thoughts. "I'm fine," she said, though she knew it wasn't entirely true. "But I'm more concerned about what's going on with Chef Anthony. Have you heard anything?"

Ethan's jaw tightened, and he glanced around the empty bakery before speaking. "There's still no sign of him. I've checked his house, his usual haunts—nothing. It's like he just vanished."

Harper's heart sank at the news. She had hoped that by now, there would have been some word, some sign that Chef Anthony was safe. But the silence only deepened the sense of foreboding that had taken root in her chest.

"Do you think something's happened to him?" she asked, her voice barely above a whisper.

"I don't know," Ethan admitted, his frustration evident. "But I'm worried. He's not the type to just disappear without a word."

Harper nodded, her mind racing. "Is there anything I can do to help?"

Ethan looked at her, his eyes filled with a mix of gratitude and something else—something that Harper couldn't quite place. "Just keep an eye out, Harper. If you notice anything unusual, anything at all, let me know."

Harper agreed, though she felt a sense of helplessness wash over her. She wanted to do more, to take action, but she didn't know where to start. "I will," she promised. "And if there's anything else I can do, anything at all, please let me know."

Ethan gave her a small nod, his expression softening slightly. "Thanks, Harper. I appreciate it."

As he turned to leave, Harper couldn't shake the feeling that they were both caught in something much bigger than they realized—something that had its roots deep in the history of Clover Grove, and perhaps even deeper in her own family's past.

When Ethan had gone, Harper stood in the middle of the bakery, the silence around her suddenly feeling oppressive. She knew she couldn't just stand by and wait for answers to come to her. If there was something she could do to help, she needed to find it. And if there were answers to be found, she would uncover them—no matter how deep they were buried.

With a renewed sense of determination, Harper set to work, her hands moving automatically as she began to prepare a new batch of dough. The familiar motions helped to calm her, to focus her thoughts, but the unease remained, lurking at the edges of her mind like a shadow that refused to be banished.

She thought about Chef Anthony, about the man she had come to know as a friend. What could have driven him to act so strangely, to disappear without a trace? Was it something personal, something he had been dealing with alone? Or was there something more, something connected to the secrets that seemed to be woven into the very fabric of Clover Grove?

Harper didn't have the answers yet, but she was determined to find them. And as she kneaded the dough, her mind began to turn over the possibilities, searching for the clues that would lead her to the truth.

The night was quiet as Harper locked up the bakery and headed upstairs to her apartment. She moved through the familiar motions of her evening routine, but her mind was elsewhere, consumed by thoughts of Chef Anthony and the mystery surrounding his disappearance.

She sat by the window, looking out at the darkened streets of Clover Grove. The town was silent, its secrets hidden in the shadows. But Harper knew that those secrets wouldn't stay buried for long. Something was stirring in Clover Grove, something that had been lying dormant for years, and it was about to come to the surface.

Harper didn't know what the future held, but she was ready to face it. She would uncover the truth, no matter what it took. And when the time came, she would be ready to confront whatever darkness lay hidden in the heart of Clover Grove.

With that thought in mind, Harper finally allowed herself to relax, the tension in her body easing as she let the comforting familiarity of her surroundings lull her to sleep. But even in sleep, the questions remained, lurking in the corners of her dreams, whispering of secrets yet to be uncovered.

And as the night wore on, those whispers grew louder, carrying with them the promise of a mystery that was far from over.

Chapter 3: The Morning After

The next morning, Harper awoke to the sound of her phone buzzing on the nightstand. She groggily reached for it, squinting at the screen to see a message from Evelyn.

"Harper, have you heard? There's something going on at Chef Anthony's restaurant. The police are everywhere."

Harper's heart skipped a beat as she sat up, wide awake now. A sense of dread washed over her, pushing away the remnants of sleep. She quickly threw on her clothes, her hands trembling as she fumbled with the buttons of her blouse. The usually comforting routine of getting dressed now felt rushed and disjointed, her mind racing with worry and a growing sense of urgency.

By the time she reached *Le Petit Boulanger*, the street was already crowded with onlookers, all craning their necks to see what was happening. The normally quiet and picturesque town square was alive with tension, the hum of concerned voices filling the air. The bakery's once welcoming façade was now a grim focal point, with yellow police tape stretched across the entrance, a stark contrast to the pastel-colored walls.

Harper pushed her way to the front of the crowd, her breath catching in her throat as she saw the cluster of police cars parked outside the restaurant. The flashing red and blue lights cast eerie shadows on the cobblestone streets, their incessant rhythm amplifying the chaos of the scene. Several officers were milling about, their expressions grim and focused as they went about their work. The sight of them, usually a source of reassurance, only heightened Harper's anxiety. This was no minor incident—something serious had happened here.

She scanned the scene, her eyes landing on Ethan near the door. He was deep in conversation with another officer, his face tense, his jaw clenched as he gave orders. His usual calm demeanor was gone, replaced by a sense of urgency and frustration. Harper hesitated, unsure if she should approach, but before she could decide, Ethan caught sight of her. His gaze softened for a brief moment before he motioned for her to come closer.

"Harper," he said, his voice low but urgent. The way he said her name, with a mix of concern and command, sent a chill down her spine. "I need you to stay back."

"What's going on?" Harper asked, her heart pounding in her chest. She could barely keep her voice steady as she spoke, the words catching in her throat. "Is Chef Anthony—"

Ethan held up a hand, cutting her off. "We're still trying to piece it together, but it doesn't look good. We found him inside—unconscious. The paramedics are working on him now, but he's in bad shape."

Harper's breath caught in her throat, a wave of nausea rolling over her. Chef Anthony, the man who had always been so full of life, so vibrant and welcoming, now lying unconscious. It was almost too much to comprehend. The image of him, bruised and battered, clashed violently with the man she knew—the man who had welcomed her to Clover Grove with open arms, who had always been ready with a smile and a laugh.

"What happened?" she managed to ask, her voice barely above a whisper.

"We're not sure yet," Ethan repeated, his voice tight with frustration. He rubbed the back of his neck, a gesture Harper had come to recognize as a sign that he was deep in thought, processing information quickly. "But from the looks of it, there was a struggle. The place was a mess when we got here. Broken glass, overturned furniture—it's clear someone was looking for something."

Harper's stomach churned. The image of the warm, welcoming restaurant she had known so well, now in disarray, filled her with a deep sense of unease. She could almost picture the scene—chairs knocked over, tables upended, glass shards glittering like malevolent stars on the floor. It was as if the heart of *Le Petit Boulanger* had been ripped out, leaving behind a hollow, chaotic shell.

"Do you think this has anything to do with the rumors Evelyn mentioned?" Harper asked, her voice trembling. "That Chef Anthony was acting strange?"

Ethan's eyes darkened, a shadow passing over his face. "It's possible. I've heard similar things from a few people in town. But until we know more, I'm not ruling anything out."

Before Harper could ask more, a paramedic emerged from the restaurant, carrying a stretcher. The crowd fell silent, a collective breath held as they watched the scene unfold. Chef Anthony lay on the stretcher, pale and unconscious, his face bruised and swollen. The sight of him, so vulnerable and diminished, was like a punch to the gut. Harper's breath hitched as she caught sight of him. The chef she remembered, always so full of life, now looked like a shadow of himself.

Ethan placed a hand on her shoulder, his touch both grounding and reassuring. "He's still alive, Harper. They're taking him to the hospital now. I'll head over there as soon as I can."

Harper's mind was spinning, a thousand thoughts and fears swirling in her head. She wanted to do something, to help in some way, but she felt completely out of her depth. "Can I come with you?" Harper asked, her voice trembling slightly. She knew she wouldn't be able to focus on anything else until she knew Chef Anthony was okay.

Ethan hesitated, clearly weighing the risks. He looked at her, his eyes searching hers as if trying to gauge her resolve. Finally, he nodded. "Alright. But stay close, and don't get involved. Let me do my job."

Harper nodded, grateful for his understanding. She knew Ethan was only trying to protect her, but she couldn't just stand by and do nothing. As they made their way to Ethan's car, Harper couldn't help but glance back at the restaurant. The once vibrant *Le Petit Boulanger* was now a crime scene, its windows reflecting the first light of dawn. Clover Grove had always felt like a safe haven, but now, that safety seemed fragile—like a thin crust ready to crack under the weight of the secrets it concealed.

The drive to the hospital was tense, the silence between them heavy with unspoken worries. Harper stared out the window, her mind racing with questions and fears. The sun was just beginning to rise, casting long, golden rays over the fields and forests that surrounded Clover Grove. But the beauty of the morning felt hollow, as if the world itself was holding its breath, waiting for something terrible to happen.

Ethan's hands gripped the steering wheel tightly, his knuckles white. Harper stole a glance at him, noticing the tension in his jaw, the way his eyes were fixed on the road ahead, unblinking. He was usually so composed, so steady, but today there was a crack in that facade—a glimpse of the weight he carried on his shoulders.

"Do you think he'll be okay?" Harper asked, her voice breaking the silence.

Ethan didn't answer right away. He let out a slow breath, his eyes briefly flicking toward her before returning to the road. "I hope so," he said finally, his voice rough with emotion. "But I've seen enough to know that we can't take anything for granted."

Harper nodded, her heart heavy. She wanted to believe that Chef Anthony would pull through, that everything would be okay in the end. But there was a part of her, a small, nagging voice in the back of her mind, that told her this was just the beginning—that there was something much darker at play.

When they arrived at the hospital, the atmosphere was just as somber. Nurses and doctors moved quickly through the halls, their expressions focused and serious. The fluorescent lights cast a harsh, clinical glow on everything, making the scene feel surreal, as if they had stepped into a different world—a world where the safety of Clover Grove was nothing more than an illusion.

Ethan led Harper to the waiting area, where a few other townsfolk had gathered, their faces etched with concern. Among them, Harper recognized Marge, the owner of the local diner, and a few of Chef Anthony's regulars. Marge, a stout woman with kind eyes and a no-nonsense attitude, approached Harper as soon as she saw her.

KNEADING THE TRUTH 25

"Harper, have you heard anything?" Marge asked, her voice tinged with worry. "Is he going to be okay?"

Harper sighed, shaking her head. "We don't know yet. He's still unconscious, and the doctors are doing what they can."

Marge's brow furrowed with concern. "That's awful. Who would want to hurt him?"

"I don't know," Harper said softly, wishing she had answers. "But I'm sure the police will figure it out."

As they waited, more people trickled into the waiting room, all hoping for news about Chef Anthony. Harper recognized many of them—regular customers from her bakery, townsfolk who had known Anthony for years. The room buzzed with low murmurs, speculations and worries shared in hushed tones. It was a strange sight, seeing so many familiar faces gathered together in such a grim setting. Harper couldn't help but feel a sense of surrealism, as if she had stepped into a nightmare she couldn't wake up from.

Eventually, Ethan returned, his expression unreadable. He motioned for Harper to step outside with him, away from the prying eyes and ears of the waiting room.

"How is he?" Harper asked as soon as they were alone in the corridor.

Ethan ran a hand through his hair, a gesture Harper was beginning to recognize as one of frustration. "He's stable, but it's going to be touch-and-go for a while. The doctors are doing what they can, but he took a pretty bad beating."

Harper's heart sank. "Do they know if he'll wake up?"

Ethan shook his head. "It's too soon to tell. But even if he does, it might be a while before he's able to talk."

Harper's mind raced with questions, but she knew now wasn't the time to ask them. She could see the weariness in Ethan's eyes, the strain of trying to hold everything together. "What do we do now?" she asked, her voice soft.

Ethan straightened, his expression determined. "We wait. I'm going back to the restaurant to continue the investigation. You should head back to the bakery, Harper. I know you want to help, but you need to keep a low profile for now."

Harper opened her mouth to protest, but the look in Ethan's eyes stopped her. He was right—she wasn't a detective, and getting too involved could put her in danger. But that didn't mean she was going to sit idly by.

"I'll go back to the bakery," she agreed, "but if I hear anything, if I remember anything that might help, I'll let you know."

Ethan's expression softened, and he gave her a small nod. "I appreciate that, Harper. Just be careful, okay?"

As they parted ways, Harper couldn't shake the feeling that the danger wasn't over. Chef Anthony's attack was just the beginning, and whatever secrets were hidden in Clover Grove, they were about to be unearthed—one way or another.

When Harper returned to the bakery, she found herself moving through the familiar routines with a kind of mechanical precision. The comforting scents of yeast and flour filled the air, but they did little to calm her nerves. Her mind was miles away, back at the hospital, back at *Le Petit Boulanger*, replaying the events of the morning over and over again.

She couldn't stop thinking about the look on Ethan's face, the tension in his voice when he spoke about the struggle at the restaurant. Something about the whole situation didn't sit right with her. It was as if they were only seeing the tip of the iceberg, with something much larger and more dangerous lurking beneath the surface.

As the afternoon wore on, Harper decided to distract herself by trying out a new recipe—a variation on her usual sourdough bread, but with a twist. She added rosemary and garlic to the dough, hoping the strong, savory flavors would help ground her, bring her back to the present. Baking had always been her refuge, her way of coping with the stresses of life. It was something she could control, something she could make right, even when everything else felt like it was falling apart.

As she worked, her thoughts kept drifting back to Chef Anthony. She wondered what he had been going through in the days leading up to the attack. Had he known he was in danger? Had he tried to reach out for help, only to find himself isolated and alone? The idea of him, a man so beloved in the community, suffering in silence, filled her with a deep sense of sorrow.

She was so lost in thought that she almost didn't hear the bell above the door jingle, signaling the arrival of a customer. Harper looked up, surprised to see Rachel Bennett, her old friend and now the town's resident food historian, stepping inside. Rachel was a petite woman with curly brown hair and bright, inquisitive eyes. She and Harper had bonded over their shared love of baking and history, and Rachel often stopped by the bakery to chat or share her latest findings.

"Hey, Harper," Rachel greeted, her tone more subdued than usual. "I heard about Chef Anthony. Is he going to be okay?"

Harper sighed, wiping her hands on a towel. "We don't know yet. He's still unconscious, and the doctors are doing what they can."

Rachel's brow furrowed with concern. "That's awful. Do they have any idea who did it?"

"Not yet," Harper said, shaking her head. "Ethan—Detective Callahan, I mean—is working on it, but there's not much to go on right now."

Rachel nodded, her expression thoughtful. "It's just so strange. I mean, who would want to hurt him? Anthony's always been so well-liked."

"That's what everyone's been saying," Harper agreed. "But I keep thinking—what if this has something to do with that secret ingredient he was looking for? The one Evelyn mentioned?"

Rachel's eyes widened with interest. "You think it could be connected?"

"I don't know," Harper admitted, "but it's the only thing that makes sense. Why else would someone ransack his restaurant and attack him?"

Rachel nodded slowly, her mind already working through the possibilities. "It's worth looking into. If Chef Anthony was onto something—something valuable—then it's possible someone else wanted it, too."

Harper's thoughts echoed Rachel's. She had a feeling that the key to this mystery lay somewhere in the history of Clover Grove, perhaps even in the old recipes and traditions that had been passed down through the generations. And if anyone could help her uncover those secrets, it was Rachel.

"Do you think you could do some digging?" Harper asked, her voice hesitant but hopeful. "Look into the history of the MacLeod Starter, maybe see if there's any connection to what Chef Anthony was researching?"

Rachel's eyes lit up with excitement. "Absolutely. I've already been curious about your family's starter—there aren't many like it, with that kind of history. I'll see what I can find."

Harper felt a small surge of relief. At least now she had someone on her side, someone who could help her uncover the truth. And while she knew it was risky, she couldn't just stand by and do nothing—not when there was so much at stake.

"Thank you, Rachel," Harper said, her voice filled with gratitude. "I really appreciate it."

"Don't mention it," Rachel replied with a grin. "This is the kind of thing I live for. And besides, I have a feeling we're onto something big."

As Rachel left the bakery, Harper felt a renewed sense of purpose. She might not be a detective, but she wasn't helpless, either. She had her skills, her knowledge of baking and history, and now she had Rachel's help, too.

And together, they were going to find out who was behind Chef Anthony's attack—and why.

As the day wore on and the sun began to set, Harper couldn't shake the feeling that they were on the brink of something big—something that could change everything they thought they knew about Clover Grove and the secrets it held. And as the first stars began to twinkle in the evening sky, she made a silent vow to herself: whatever it took, she would uncover the truth.

Chapter 4: A Town on Edge

The ride to the hospital was tense, the silence between Harper and Ethan heavy with unspoken worries. Harper stared out the window, her mind racing with questions. What had happened to Chef Anthony? Who could have done this, and why? And more importantly, what had they been searching for? The gentle roll of the car's tires on the road did little to soothe her; each bump felt like an echo of the turmoil inside her.

Ethan's hands gripped the steering wheel tightly, his knuckles white with the pressure. He was usually so composed, so in control, but today there was a tension in him that Harper hadn't seen before. She stole glances at him, trying to read the emotions flickering across his face, but his expression was unreadable—a mask of professionalism hiding whatever thoughts churned beneath the surface.

When they arrived at the hospital, the atmosphere was just as somber as Harper had feared. Nurses and doctors moved quickly through the halls, their expressions focused and serious. The sterile scent of disinfectant filled the air, mingling with the quiet hum of hospital machinery. It was a stark contrast to the warmth and familiarity of Clover Grove, a reminder that the town was not immune to the harsh realities of the world.

Ethan led Harper to the waiting area, where a few other townsfolk had gathered, their faces etched with concern. The small, beige-colored room was packed with people who had known Chef Anthony for years—friends, colleagues, and customers who had all been touched by his kindness. The usual murmur of polite conversation was absent, replaced by a heavy, uneasy silence that seemed to weigh down on everyone present.

Among them, Harper recognized Marge, the owner of the local diner, and a few of Chef Anthony's regulars. Marge, a stout woman with kind eyes and a no-nonsense attitude, approached Harper as soon as she saw her. Her face was lined with worry, her usually bright demeanor dimmed by the weight of the situation.

"Harper, have you heard anything?" Marge asked, her voice tinged with worry. She wrung her hands together, a nervous habit Harper had never seen in her before.

"Not much," Harper admitted, glancing at Ethan, who had stepped away to speak with a doctor. She watched as he conferred with the medical staff, his expression serious and intent. "He's still unconscious, but they're doing everything they can."

Marge sighed heavily, her shoulders slumping as if the weight of the world had settled on them. "I just can't believe it. Anthony's such a good man. Who would want to hurt him?"

"I don't know," Harper said softly, wishing she had answers. She had always admired Chef Anthony—not just for his culinary skills, but for the way he made everyone around him feel special, as if they were the most important person in the room. The idea that someone would want to harm him was unthinkable.

"But I'm sure the police will figure it out," she added, trying to sound reassuring, though she wasn't sure if she believed it herself. The look in Ethan's eyes had told her that this was no ordinary case, that there were layers to this mystery that had yet to be uncovered.

As they waited, more people trickled into the waiting room, all hoping for news about Chef Anthony. Harper recognized many of them—regular customers from her bakery, townsfolk who had known Anthony for years. The room buzzed with low murmurs, speculations and worries shared in hushed tones. It was as if the whole town had been shaken by the incident, their usual sense of security shattered by the violence that had touched one of their own.

Harper found herself caught in snippets of conversation as people speculated on what could have happened. "It's got to be someone from out of town," one man said. "No one here would do such a thing." Another woman whispered, "I heard he was mixed up in something. Maybe this was payback." The words hung in the air, heavy and foreboding, as Harper's mind spun with the implications.

Eventually, Ethan returned, his expression unreadable. He motioned for Harper to step outside with him, away from the prying eyes and ears of the waiting room. She followed him out into the corridor, the fluorescent lights casting harsh shadows on the walls.

"How is he?" Harper asked as soon as they were alone, her voice barely above a whisper. The tension in her body was almost unbearable, like a taut string ready to snap.

Ethan ran a hand through his hair, a gesture Harper was beginning to recognize as one of frustration. "He's stable, but it's going to be touch-and-go for a while. The doctors are doing what they can, but he took a pretty bad beating."

Harper's heart sank. The idea of Chef Anthony, always so strong and full of life, lying unconscious and vulnerable in a hospital bed was almost too much to bear. "Do they know if he'll wake up?" she asked, her voice trembling.

Ethan shook his head, his jaw tightening. "It's too soon to tell. But even if he does, it might be a while before he's able to talk."

Harper's mind raced. If Chef Anthony couldn't speak, then how would they ever find out what happened to him? What had he been involved in that led to this? And more importantly, was he still in danger? The questions swirled around in her head, each one more urgent than the last.

As if reading her thoughts, Ethan added, "We've got officers posted at his room. Whoever did this might try to finish the job, and we're not taking any chances."

Harper nodded, though the reassurance did little to calm her nerves. "What do we do now?" she asked, her voice steady despite the turmoil inside her.

Ethan hesitated, then said, "We wait. I'll be going back to the restaurant to continue the investigation. You should head back to the bakery, Harper. I know you want to help, but you need to keep a low profile for now."

Harper opened her mouth to protest, but the look in Ethan's eyes stopped her. He was right—she wasn't a detective, and getting too involved could put her in danger. But that didn't mean she was going to sit idly by.

"I'll go back to the bakery," she agreed, "but if I hear anything, if I remember anything that might help, I'll let you know."

Ethan's expression softened, and he gave her a small nod. "I appreciate that, Harper. Just be careful, okay?"

As they parted ways, Harper couldn't shake the feeling that the danger wasn't over. Chef Anthony's attack was just the beginning, and whatever secrets were hidden in Clover Grove, they were about to be unearthed—one way or another.

On her way back to the bakery, Harper couldn't stop the questions from flooding her mind. What had Chef Anthony been involved in? Was it something from his past that had caught up with him, or was it something more recent? She thought about the rumors Evelyn had mentioned, about Anthony acting strangely, about the secret ingredient he'd been searching for. Could it be connected?

By the time she reached the bakery, Harper's thoughts were a tangled mess. She unlocked the door and stepped inside, the familiar scents of yeast and flour greeting her like old friends. Normally, the bakery was a place of comfort for her, a sanctuary where she could escape the world's problems. But today, it felt different—tainted by the uncertainty and fear that had settled over Clover Grove like a dark cloud.

Harper went through the motions of preparing for the day, but her heart wasn't in it. Her mind kept drifting back to the hospital, to Chef Anthony lying unconscious in a sterile bed, surrounded by machines and monitors. She wished she could do something, anything, to help. But all she could do was wait and hope that the answers would come to them.

As the morning passed, the bakery began to fill with customers, but the usual lively chatter was muted, replaced by hushed conversations and worried glances. It was clear that the whole town was on edge, their sense of security shattered by the attack on one of their own. Harper did her best to keep up appearances, smiling and chatting with her customers, but inside, she was struggling to keep it together.

Around midday, Harper decided to take a break. She made herself a cup of coffee and sat down at one of the small tables by the window, gazing out at the bustling street. The sun was shining, and the sky was a clear, bright blue, but the beauty of the day felt hollow, as if it were mocking the fear and uncertainty that had gripped Clover Grove.

As she sipped her coffee, Harper's thoughts drifted to Rachel and the research she had promised to do on the MacLeod Starter. If there was any connection between the starter and what had happened to Chef Anthony, Rachel might be able to find it. The thought gave Harper a small glimmer of hope, something to hold onto in the midst of the chaos.

The bell above the door jingled, pulling Harper from her thoughts. She looked up to see Amelia Thornton stepping inside. Amelia was a tall, slender woman with long, dark hair and striking blue eyes that always seemed to be watching, calculating. She had been a close friend of Chef Anthony's, often helping him out at the restaurant when he needed an extra pair of hands.

"Amelia," Harper greeted, her voice tinged with surprise. "I didn't expect to see you today."

Amelia offered a small, tight-lipped smile as she approached the counter. "I've been keeping to myself lately. Too much going on, you know?"

Harper nodded, understanding the sentiment all too well. "I'm glad you stopped by. How are you holding up?"

Amelia sighed, her expression turning somber. "It's been tough. Anthony's like family to me, and seeing him like this... it's hard. But I've been thinking a lot about what happened, and I wanted to talk to you."

Harper's interest piqued. "What about?"

Amelia hesitated, glancing around the empty bakery as if checking to make sure they were alone. "It's about Anthony—what he was working on before the attack. He was obsessed with finding something, a recipe or an ingredient, I'm not sure. But he kept saying it was the key to everything."

Harper's heart skipped a beat. "The key to what?"

"I don't know," Amelia admitted, her voice low. "But whatever it was, it consumed him. He was always at the restaurant, staying late, poring over old books and notes. He barely slept, barely ate. I tried to get him to talk about it, but he just kept saying that he was close, that he couldn't stop now."

Harper felt a chill run down her spine. "Do you think it had something to do with the MacLeod Starter?"

Amelia's eyes flickered with uncertainty. "It's possible. He mentioned your name a few times, said something about the starter being special, unique. But he wouldn't tell me more than that. It was like he was afraid to say too much."

Harper's mind raced with possibilities. If Chef Anthony had been onto something—something connected to her family's starter—then whoever had attacked him might still be after it.

"Thank you for telling me this," Harper said, her voice filled with sincerity. "It means a lot."

Amelia nodded, her expression serious. "Just be careful, Harper. Whatever Anthony was involved in, it's dangerous. And I have a feeling it's far from over."

As Amelia left the bakery, Harper felt a knot of anxiety tighten in her chest. The more she learned about Chef Anthony's obsession, the more she realized just how deep this mystery went. And the more she understood that the danger was growing closer with each passing day.

Harper knew she couldn't sit idly by. There was too much at stake—too many unanswered questions, too many lives at risk. She needed to take action, to dig deeper into the mystery of the MacLeod Starter and the secrets it held.

But as she set to work on her next batch of dough, Harper couldn't shake the feeling that she was being watched. She glanced out the window, but the street was empty, the usual bustle of midday Clover Grove strangely subdued. The feeling of being observed persisted, however, a nagging sensation that prickled at the back of her neck.

She tried to focus on her work, kneading the dough with more force than necessary, but the unease lingered. What if Amelia was right? What if the danger wasn't over? What if it was only just beginning?

As the afternoon wore on, Harper found herself growing more and more anxious. She kept glancing over her shoulder, half-expecting to see someone standing in the doorway, watching her. But each time she looked, the bakery was empty, the only sounds the soft hum of the refrigerator and the occasional creak of the old wooden floorboards.

When the last customer had left and the bakery was finally quiet, Harper decided to close up early. She couldn't shake the feeling that something was about to happen, that the peace of Clover Grove was about to be shattered once again.

She locked the door behind her and headed upstairs to her apartment, her mind still racing with questions and fears. She needed to talk to Rachel, to find out if she had uncovered anything about the MacLeod Starter that could help them make sense of what was happening.

But even as she made her way to her small, cozy apartment, Harper couldn't shake the feeling that she wasn't alone. The shadows seemed to move with her, stretching out as if trying to reach her, to pull her into their depths. She quickened her pace, her heart pounding in her chest, until she finally reached the safety of her apartment.

Inside, she locked the door behind her and leaned against it, her breath coming in short, shaky gasps. The apartment was dark, the only light coming from the streetlamp outside her window, casting long shadows across the floor. She stood there for a moment, trying to calm her racing heart, but the unease refused to leave her.

She walked over to the window and looked out at the quiet street below. The town was bathed in the soft glow of the streetlights, the shadows long and deep. But there was nothing out of the ordinary, no sign of the danger she felt lurking just out of sight.

Harper sighed and turned away from the window. She needed to clear her head, to focus on what she could do to help. Tomorrow, she would talk to Rachel, and together they would dig deeper into the mystery of the MacLeod Starter. They would find out what Chef Anthony had been searching for, and why someone had been willing to hurt him to get it.

But for now, all she could do was wait. And hope that when the time came, she would be ready to face whatever darkness lay ahead.

As Harper prepared for bed, she couldn't shake the feeling that she was standing on the edge of something big—something that could change everything she thought she knew about Clover Grove, and about herself. And as she lay in bed, staring up at the ceiling, she made a silent vow to herself: whatever it took, she would uncover the truth.

But as sleep finally claimed her, the shadows outside her window seemed to grow darker, deeper, as if they were waiting for something—or someone—to emerge from their depths. And in the quiet of the night, the town of Clover Grove held its breath, waiting for the secrets it had buried for so long to finally come to light.

Chapter 5: Hidden in the Dough

Back at "The Yeast of Time," Harper tried to focus on her work, but her thoughts kept drifting back to Chef Anthony and the mystery surrounding his attack. The bakery, usually a hub of activity, was unusually quiet, the steady stream of customers slowed to a trickle as word of the incident spread through town. Those who did come in were subdued, their usual chatter replaced by concerned whispers. The air, once filled with the comforting scent of fresh bread and pastries, now seemed heavy with unease.

As Harper prepared a new batch of dough, her hands moved automatically, kneading the soft, elastic mass with practiced ease. The dough responded to her touch, stretching and folding just as it should, but her mind was elsewhere, replaying her last conversation with Chef Anthony. He had been his usual cheerful self, but now that she thought about it, there had been something in his eyes—a hint of worry, perhaps, or distraction that she hadn't noticed at the time. It was as if he had been carrying a burden that he hadn't wanted to share, and now Harper was left to wonder what that burden had been.

The rhythmic motion of kneading usually brought Harper a sense of calm, a way to center herself when the world around her felt chaotic. But today, no matter how hard she tried, she couldn't shake the feeling that something was terribly wrong. Her mind kept circling back to the same questions: What had Anthony been involved in? Why had someone attacked him? And most troubling of all, was there more danger lurking in the shadows?

The bell above the door jingled, pulling Harper from her thoughts. She looked up to see Rachel Bennett, her old friend and now the town's resident food historian, stepping inside. Rachel was a petite woman with curly brown hair and bright, inquisitive eyes that always seemed to be on the verge of discovering something fascinating. She and Harper had bonded over their shared love of baking and history, and Rachel often stopped by the bakery to chat or share her latest findings. But today, Rachel's usual exuberance was tempered, her expression mirroring the town's collective anxiety.

"Hey, Harper," Rachel greeted, her tone more subdued than usual. The corners of her mouth lifted in a small, sympathetic smile, but it didn't reach her eyes. "I heard about Chef Anthony. Is he going to be okay?"

Harper sighed, wiping her hands on a towel as she stepped away from the dough. "We don't know yet. He's still unconscious, and the doctors are doing what they can. It's just so hard to believe—Anthony, of all people."

Rachel's brow furrowed with concern. "That's awful. Do they have any idea who did it? Why would anyone want to hurt him?"

"Not yet," Harper said, shaking her head. She glanced toward the back of the bakery, where the scent of baking bread wafted through the air, mingling with the tension that seemed to have settled over everything. "Ethan—Detective Callahan, I mean—is working on it, but there's not much to go on right now."

Rachel nodded, her expression thoughtful. "It's just so strange. I mean, who would want to hurt him? Anthony's always been so well-liked. It doesn't make any sense."

"That's what everyone's been saying," Harper agreed, her voice tinged with frustration. She leaned against the counter, her arms crossed over her chest. "But I keep thinking—what if this has something to do with that secret ingredient he was looking for? The one Evelyn mentioned?"

Rachel's eyes widened with interest, a spark of curiosity igniting in their depths. "You think it could be connected? That whatever he was searching for might have led to this?"

"I don't know," Harper admitted, her voice tinged with uncertainty. "But it's the only thing that makes sense. Why else would someone ransack his restaurant and attack him?"

Rachel nodded slowly, her mind already working through the possibilities. Harper could practically see the wheels turning in her friend's head, the pieces of the puzzle beginning to come together. "It's worth looking into. If Chef Anthony was onto something—something valuable—then it's possible someone else wanted it, too."

Harper's thoughts echoed Rachel's. She had a feeling that the key to this mystery lay somewhere in the history of Clover Grove, perhaps even in the old recipes and traditions that had been passed down through the generations. And if anyone could help her uncover those secrets, it was Rachel.

"Do you think you could do some digging?" Harper asked, her voice hesitant but hopeful. She knew she was asking a lot, but Rachel was the only person she trusted to take on this task. "Look into the history of the MacLeod Starter, maybe see if there's any connection to what Chef Anthony was researching?"

Rachel's eyes lit up with excitement, her earlier somberness giving way to the thrill of a new challenge. "Absolutely. I've already been curious about your family's starter—there aren't many like it, with that kind of history. I'll see what I can find."

Harper felt a small surge of relief. At least now she had someone on her side, someone who could help her uncover the truth. And while she knew it was risky, she couldn't just stand by and do nothing—not when there was so much at stake. The thought of Rachel digging through old records, uncovering long-forgotten secrets, gave Harper a sense of hope that had been missing since the incident.

"Thank you, Rachel," Harper said, her voice filled with gratitude. "I really appreciate it. And if you find anything, anything at all, let me know right away."

"Don't mention it," Rachel replied with a grin. "This is the kind of thing I live for. And besides, I have a feeling we're onto something big."

As Rachel left the bakery, Harper felt a renewed sense of purpose. She might not be a detective, but she wasn't helpless, either. She had her skills, her knowledge of baking and history, and now she had Rachel's help, too.

And together, they were going to find out who was behind Chef Anthony's attack—and why.

As the day wore on, Harper threw herself into her work, hoping to find solace in the familiar rhythms of baking. She prepared batch after batch of dough, her hands moving with practiced precision, but her mind remained restless, unable to shake the questions that had been haunting her since the attack.

She thought about the MacLeod Starter, the living, breathing link to her ancestors that had been passed down through generations. It was more than just a recipe; it was a piece of history, a legacy that Harper had been entrusted to protect. And now, it seemed, that legacy might be at the center of something much larger and more dangerous than she had ever imagined.

The thought filled her with a sense of unease. What if the starter was more than just a family heirloom? What if it held some kind of power or secret that others would do anything to possess? The idea seemed far-fetched, almost like something out of a mystery novel, but Harper couldn't dismiss it entirely. There were too many unanswered questions, too many strange coincidences that seemed to point to something bigger.

As she shaped the dough into loaves, Harper's mind drifted back to her grandmother, Fiona MacLeod, who had passed the starter down to her. Fiona had always spoken of the starter with a kind of reverence, as if it were a sacred object. She had told Harper stories of how the starter had sustained their family through hard times, how it had been a source of comfort and strength for generations. But Fiona had also hinted at something more, something she had never fully explained—a mystery that had always intrigued Harper but had never seemed important until now.

Harper could still remember the way Fiona's eyes had sparkled with mischief as she recounted tales of their ancestors in the Scottish Highlands, of how the starter had been kept alive through wars and famines, passed down from mother to daughter like a precious jewel. But there had been one story that had always stood out to Harper, a story that had seemed more like a fairy tale than history.

Fiona had spoken of a time, long ago, when the MacLeods had been known not just for their baking, but for their knowledge of herbs and healing. They had been respected and feared in equal measure, for it was said that the women of the family possessed a gift—a gift that was somehow tied to the starter. According to the legend, the starter was more than just a mixture of flour and water; it was infused with the essence of the Highlands, with the power of the earth itself. And those who knew how to harness that power could use it for great good—or great evil.

Harper had always dismissed the story as just that—a story, a bit of folklore passed down through the generations. But now, with everything that had happened, she couldn't help but wonder if there was some truth to it. What if the starter did have some kind of power? And what if Chef Anthony had discovered that power—or worse, what if someone else had?

The thought sent a shiver down her spine. She glanced at the jar of starter sitting on the counter, its surface bubbling and alive, and felt a strange sense of foreboding. She had always taken the starter for granted, seen it as a part of her family's history, but now she was beginning to see it in a new light—as something mysterious, something that might be more than she had ever imagined.

The bell above the door jingled again, and Harper looked up to see Detective Ethan Callahan stepping inside. His presence brought a sense of both relief and tension. Relief because she trusted him and believed he was doing everything he could to solve this mystery; tension because his arrival meant that the situation might be escalating.

"Ethan," Harper greeted, her voice laced with surprise. "I didn't expect to see you so soon. Is there any news?"

Ethan's expression was serious, his eyes scanning the bakery as if assessing it for potential threats. He approached the counter, his movements deliberate and measured. "We're still piecing things together," he said, his tone cautious. "But I wanted to check in with you, see how you're holding up."

"I'm managing," Harper replied, though she knew her voice didn't carry much conviction. She could feel the weight of the situation pressing down on her, making it hard to focus, hard to breathe. "It's just... everything feels so uncertain right now."

Ethan nodded, his gaze softening slightly as he looked at her. "I understand. But I need you to stay strong, Harper. We're doing everything we can to keep the town safe, and that includes you."

Harper appreciated his words, but they did little to quell the anxiety gnawing at her insides. "Do you really think this could be connected to the MacLeod Starter?" she asked, voicing the question that had been plaguing her for hours.

Ethan hesitated, his eyes narrowing slightly as he considered her words. "It's possible," he admitted, though his tone was guarded. "There's a lot we don't know yet, but we can't rule anything out."

Harper nodded, though the uncertainty of his response only heightened her fears. "Rachel's going to do some research, see if she can find any connections in the history of the starter. Maybe that will give us some answers."

Ethan's expression brightened at the mention of Rachel. "That's a good idea. Rachel's got a knack for finding things others might overlook. If there's something to be uncovered, she'll find it."

"I hope so," Harper said softly, her gaze drifting to the jar of starter on the counter. "I just wish we knew what we were dealing with."

"We will," Ethan said, his voice filled with quiet determination. "It's just going to take time. And in the meantime, I need you to be careful, Harper. If anything seems off, if you notice anything unusual, don't hesitate to call me."

"I will," Harper promised, though the thought of being in danger made her stomach churn. "But I'm not going to sit back and do nothing, either. I want to help."

Ethan smiled, though there was a hint of worry in his eyes. "I know you do. Just promise me you'll be careful."

Harper nodded, her resolve hardening. "I promise."

As Ethan left the bakery, Harper felt a renewed sense of determination. She wasn't going to let fear hold her back. She was going to find out the truth about what had happened to Chef Anthony, and about the secrets hidden in the MacLeod Starter.

But as she returned to her work, the sense of unease lingered, like a shadow that refused to be banished. The starter, once a source of comfort and pride, now seemed to hold secrets of its own—secrets that Harper was determined to uncover, no matter the cost.

Chapter 6: A Knot of Secrets

The following days passed in a haze of worry and tension. Harper kept the bakery running as best she could, but her mind was constantly elsewhere, distracted by the unfolding mystery. The usually comforting routine of mixing, kneading, and baking now felt like a fragile thread tethering her to reality, as her thoughts constantly drifted back to Chef Anthony and the strange events surrounding his attack.

Customers came in with updates—rumors about Chef Anthony's condition, speculation about who might have attacked him, and theories about what had been stolen from the restaurant. The once lively chatter of the bakery had transformed into a quiet, almost somber atmosphere, where everyone seemed to be walking on eggshells, as if the very air in Clover Grove had become thick with unease.

Through it all, Ethan kept Harper updated on the investigation, though there was little new information to share. The police had found no fingerprints, no trace of the intruder, and Chef Anthony remained unconscious, unable to provide any answers. The lack of progress was frustrating for everyone, but especially for Harper, who felt as though she was living in a fog, unable to see the path forward.

One afternoon, as Harper was rolling out dough for a new batch of sourdough loaves, her phone buzzed with a message. It was from Rachel.

"Harper, I found something. Can you meet me at the library after you close up?"

Harper's heart raced with anticipation as she quickly replied, agreeing to meet her friend. She finished her work for the day, her movements brisk and efficient as she cleaned up the bakery and locked the doors. The sky outside had turned a soft shade of pink, the sun beginning its descent, casting long shadows across the quiet streets of Clover Grove.

As she made her way to the Clover Grove Public Library, Harper's mind buzzed with possibilities. What had Rachel found? Could it be the key to understanding what had happened to Chef Anthony? And more importantly, could it help them figure out who was responsible?

The library was housed in a grand old building, its stone walls and arched windows giving it an air of timeless wisdom. Inside, the scent of old books and polished wood filled the air, and the soft sound of pages turning provided a soothing backdrop to the otherwise quiet space. Harper had always loved the library, with its labyrinthine shelves and cozy reading nooks, but today it felt different—charged with a sense of purpose that matched her own urgency.

Rachel was waiting for Harper in the library's archive room, a secluded space filled with stacks of old books and papers. The room was dimly lit, the warm glow of a desk lamp illuminating the dust motes that danced in the air. Rachel looked up as Harper entered, her eyes bright with excitement, a stark contrast to the seriousness of their situation.

"Harper, you're not going to believe what I found," Rachel said, her voice hushed with urgency. She gestured to the table in front of her, where an old, leather-bound book lay open, its pages yellowed with age.

Harper moved to stand beside her, her heart pounding with anticipation. "What is it?" she asked, leaning in to get a closer look.

Rachel pointed to the open book. The handwriting was elegant but faded, the ink barely visible in some places, but the words were clear enough to read.

"This is an old recipe book I found in the archives," Rachel explained, her voice tinged with excitement. "It's dated back to the 1800s, and it belonged to one of the early settlers of Clover Grove. But what's interesting is this."

She flipped to a page near the middle of the book, where a recipe for sourdough bread was written in neat script. The ingredients were simple—flour, water, salt, and sourdough starter—but there was a note scribbled in the margin, written in a different hand.

"The key lies in the yeast—an old strain, passed down through the generations. A gift from the Highlands, where bread was more than sustenance. Guard it well."

Harper's breath caught in her throat as she read the words. "That sounds like it could be connected to my family's starter."

"That's what I thought," Rachel said, her voice filled with excitement. She pushed the book closer to Harper, as if sharing a precious secret. "I did some more digging, and I found references to a similar strain of yeast used by your ancestors in Scotland. It was said to have special properties—something about how it was cultivated in the Highlands, where the air was different, purer. People believed it had healing properties, that it could ward off illness."

Harper's mind raced as she processed the information. Could this be what Chef Anthony had been after? The secret of the MacLeod Starter, a strain of yeast with supposed magical properties? The idea seemed almost fantastical, but given everything that had happened, Harper was willing to believe anything.

"But why would someone attack Chef Anthony over this?" Harper asked, her voice tinged with confusion. "I mean, it's just yeast, right?"

Rachel shrugged, though her expression remained thoughtful. "Maybe. Or maybe there's more to it—something we don't know yet. If Chef Anthony was trying to replicate the starter, or if he thought it could make his bread more valuable, someone else might have wanted it too."

Harper nodded slowly, the pieces of the puzzle beginning to fall into place. "So, you think someone might have attacked him to steal the secret? To get their hands on the starter?"

"It's possible," Rachel said. She leaned back in her chair, her brow furrowed as she considered the implications. "And if that's the case, then whoever did this might still be looking for it."

Harper felt a chill run down her spine. The idea that someone might come after her—or her family's starter—was terrifying. But it also made her more determined than ever to find out the truth. She had inherited the starter from her grandmother, along with the responsibility of protecting it. And now it seemed that responsibility was more important than ever.

"Thank you, Rachel," Harper said, her voice filled with gratitude. "This is a huge help. But we need to be careful. If someone's willing to hurt Chef Anthony over this, we could be next."

Rachel nodded, her expression serious. "Agreed. But I'm not backing down. We're going to figure this out, Harper. Together."

The two women sat in silence for a moment, the weight of the situation settling over them like a heavy blanket. The library, usually a place of comfort and quiet contemplation, now felt like a battleground, with the old books and documents surrounding them like silent witnesses to the unfolding drama.

As they left the library, Harper couldn't help but feel a sense of foreboding. The mystery was growing more complex by the day, and the danger was only increasing. But she also knew that she wasn't alone. With Rachel by her side, and Ethan working on the case, she had allies she could trust.

The walk back to the bakery was quiet, the evening air cool against Harper's skin. The streets of Clover Grove were mostly deserted, the shops closed and the townsfolk indoors, as if the entire town had retreated into itself, waiting for the storm to pass. But Harper knew that this storm was only just beginning.

When she reached the bakery, Harper hesitated before unlocking the door. The building, usually a place of warmth and safety, now seemed to hold its own secrets, shadows lurking in the corners of her mind. She took a deep breath, trying to shake off the feeling, and stepped inside.

The bakery was dark and quiet, the scents of the day's baking still lingering in the air. Harper flipped on the lights, the warm glow chasing away the shadows, but not the unease that had settled in her chest. She walked over to the counter, her gaze falling on the jar of sourdough starter that sat in its usual place.

KNEADING THE TRUTH 53

She stared at it for a long moment, her thoughts swirling. This simple jar, filled with a bubbling mixture of flour and water, held the key to so much—her family's history, their traditions, and now, it seemed, a mystery that had the power to bring harm to those she cared about. It was a lot to take in, and for a moment, Harper felt overwhelmed.

She reached out and touched the jar, the cool glass grounding her in the present. The starter was alive, a living link to her ancestors, and now it was her responsibility to protect it. But how could she protect something when she didn't even understand what made it so valuable?

Harper knew she needed to talk to Ethan, to share what she and Rachel had discovered. But part of her hesitated. The more people who knew about the starter, the more dangerous the situation could become. And yet, keeping it a secret didn't seem like an option either—not when lives were at stake.

She sighed, rubbing her temples as she tried to clear her mind. The answers were out there, somewhere, buried in the history of her family, in the old recipes and stories that had been passed down through the generations. But uncovering those answers wouldn't be easy, and it wouldn't be without risk.

As Harper prepared to close up for the night, she couldn't shake the feeling that she was being watched. The sensation was subtle, like a whisper of wind on the back of her neck, but it was enough to make her glance over her shoulder, her heart skipping a beat. But the bakery was empty, the only sounds the soft hum of the refrigerator and the distant creak of the floorboards.

She shook her head, trying to dismiss the feeling as paranoia. But as she locked the door and headed upstairs to her apartment, the unease lingered, like a shadow that refused to be banished. She knew that the mystery surrounding the MacLeod Starter was far from over, and that whatever secrets it held, they were about to be brought to light—whether she was ready for them or not.

As Harper settled into bed that night, her thoughts were a tangled knot of worry and determination. She had always been good at unraveling puzzles, at finding the truth hidden beneath layers of secrecy. But this puzzle was different—more personal, more dangerous. And the stakes were higher than they had ever been before.

But Harper also knew that she wasn't alone. With Rachel and Ethan by her side, she had allies she could trust, people who would help her uncover the truth, no matter how deep it was buried. And together, they were going to solve this mystery—no matter the cost.

Chapter 7: The Taste of Fear

The next morning, Harper arrived at the bakery earlier than usual. The air was crisp with the first hints of autumn, and the sky was a soft, pale blue, promising a clear day ahead. But despite the beauty of the morning, Harper's thoughts were clouded with worry. She had barely slept the night before, her mind too full of questions and possibilities. The idea that someone might be after her family's starter—a recipe that had been passed down for generations—was both terrifying and surreal. But the evidence was mounting, and she couldn't ignore it.

As she prepared to open the bakery, Harper decided to try something new. She had been experimenting with different ways to use sourdough discard, the portion of the starter that was typically thrown away during the feeding process. The waste always bothered her; it seemed like such a shame to throw away something that still had so much potential. Over time, she'd discovered that the discard could be used in all sorts of recipes, from pancakes to crackers. Each new recipe felt like a small victory, a way to honor her family's legacy by making sure nothing was wasted.

Today, she decided to make sourdough discard brownies—a rich, chocolatey treat that would appeal to her customers and help use up some of the extra starter. She mixed the ingredients together, enjoying the familiar rhythm of baking as she tried to push her worries aside. The act of baking had always been her solace, a way to center herself when the world outside felt chaotic. The warmth of the kitchen, the soothing scent of vanilla and chocolate, the feel of the dough in her hands—all of it worked together to calm her racing thoughts.

As the brownies baked, filling the bakery with the comforting scent of chocolate and vanilla, the bell above the door jingled, and Harper looked up to see Ethan Callahan stepping inside. His presence was unexpected, but not unwelcome. Over the past few days, Ethan had become a steadying force in her life, someone she could rely on even as everything else seemed to be spiraling out of control.

"Morning, Detective," Harper greeted, trying to keep her tone light. "What brings you here so early?"

Ethan offered her a small smile, though his eyes remained serious. He had the look of a man who hadn't slept much either, dark circles under his eyes betraying his fatigue. "I was in the area and thought I'd check in. How are you holding up?"

Harper shrugged, turning her attention back to the brownies as she removed them from the oven. The rich scent filled the air, momentarily pushing away her worries. "I'm okay, considering. Just trying to keep busy." She began cutting the brownies into neat squares, her movements precise and deliberate, as if focusing on the task could somehow bring order to the chaos in her mind.

Ethan leaned against the counter, watching her with an unreadable expression. "I heard about your visit to the library yesterday. Rachel told me you found something interesting."

Harper nodded, setting the knife down and turning to face him. "We did. She found an old recipe book that mentioned a special strain of yeast—one that sounds a lot like the MacLeod Starter."

Ethan's expression grew more serious, his brows knitting together in thought. "And you think that's what this is all about? Someone trying to get their hands on your family's starter?"

"It's possible," Harper said, though her tone was uncertain. The whole situation still felt surreal, like something out of a novel rather than her own life. "But I don't understand why someone would go to such lengths. I mean, it's just bread, right?"

"Maybe," Ethan replied, his voice thoughtful as he considered the possibilities. "But people do crazy things for less. If someone believes that starter is valuable, or if they think it could give them an edge, they might be willing to do anything to get it."

Harper shivered at the thought. The idea that someone could be so obsessed with her family's legacy that they'd resort to violence was chilling. "So what do we do now?"

Ethan straightened, his expression determined, the familiar look of a man who was ready to face whatever challenges lay ahead. "We keep looking. I'm going to talk to a few more people in town, see if anyone else has noticed anything unusual. In the meantime, I want you to be careful, Harper. Don't go anywhere alone, and if you notice anything out of the ordinary, call me immediately."

Harper nodded, her heart heavy with worry. "I will. And Ethan—thank you. For everything." The gratitude in her voice was genuine. In a situation where so much felt out of her control, knowing that Ethan was in her corner made all the difference.

Ethan's expression softened, and he gave her a reassuring smile. "It's my job, Harper. And besides, I'm not about to let anything happen to you." There was a warmth in his voice that hadn't been there before, a hint of something more than just professional concern. It was a connection that had been growing between them, subtle but undeniable.

As he left the bakery, Harper couldn't help but feel a small flicker of warmth in her chest. Despite the danger, despite the uncertainty, she was grateful to have someone like Ethan looking out for her. She watched him walk down the street, his figure gradually disappearing into the early morning mist. For a moment, she allowed herself to imagine what it might be like if things were different—if they weren't caught up in a mystery that seemed to grow more dangerous by the day.

But as she turned her attention back to the brownies, a nagging voice in the back of her mind reminded her that this was far from over. The mystery of the MacLeod Starter was deeper than she had ever imagined, and the danger was closer than she cared to admit. She could feel it, like a shadow lurking just out of sight, waiting for the right moment to strike.

The day passed in a blur of activity. Customers came and went, their faces a mix of curiosity and concern as they asked Harper about Chef Anthony's condition and speculated on who could have done such a thing. Harper answered their questions as best she could, but the truth was, she had no more answers than they did.

By the time the afternoon rolled around, Harper was exhausted, both physically and mentally. She took a moment to sit down, her hands aching from hours of kneading dough and

KNEADING THE TRUTH

rolling out pastries. The bakery was quiet now, the last of the morning rush long gone, leaving her alone with her thoughts.

She found herself staring at the jar of starter on the counter, the bubbling mixture that had caused so much trouble. It was hard to believe that something so simple, so ordinary, could hold such significance. And yet, the more she learned, the more she realized that the starter was anything but ordinary.

The bell above the door jingled again, and Harper looked up, expecting to see another customer. But instead, it was Rachel, her face flushed with excitement as she hurried inside.

"Harper, I've found something else," Rachel said, her voice breathless with anticipation.

Harper's exhaustion vanished in an instant, replaced by a surge of adrenaline. "What is it?" she asked, standing up and moving toward her friend.

Rachel pulled a folded piece of paper from her bag and handed it to Harper. "I was going through some more of the old records at the library, and I came across this. It's a letter—dated back to the late 1800s, from a man named Angus MacLeod."

"Angus MacLeod?" Harper repeated, recognizing the name as one of her ancestors. She unfolded the paper carefully, her eyes scanning the faded script.

"To my dearest daughter," the letter began. "There is something you must know about the starter. It is not merely a recipe—it is a trust, passed down through our family for generations. It holds the essence of our heritage, our strength. Guard it well, for there are those who would seek to take it for themselves, to use it for their own gain. Beware the shadows that linger at our door, for they have come before, and they will come again."

Harper's hands trembled as she read the words. The letter was a warning, a message from the past that seemed eerily relevant to the present. She looked up at Rachel, her heart pounding in her chest.

"This... this changes everything," Harper said, her voice barely above a whisper. The letter confirmed what she had feared—that the starter was more than just a family heirloom. It was a powerful secret, one that had been guarded by her ancestors for centuries.

"I know," Rachel agreed, her expression serious. "But it also means we're on the right track. Whatever's happening now, it's connected to this—to your family's past."

Harper nodded, her mind racing. "We need to figure out who's behind this. If they're after the starter, they won't stop until they get it."

Rachel's eyes narrowed with determination. "Then we'll just have to stay one step ahead of them."

The two women stood in silence for a moment, the weight of the situation settling over them like a heavy fog. But Harper knew that they couldn't afford to hesitate. The stakes were too high, and time was running out.

As the afternoon sun dipped lower in the sky, casting long shadows across the floor of the bakery, Harper made a decision. She was going to protect her family's legacy, no matter what it took. And she wasn't going to let fear hold her back.

Harper looked at Rachel, a sense of resolve settling over her. "Let's get to work."

Chapter 8: Stirring the Pot

The next few days passed in a tense blur. Harper kept the bakery running as usual, but the atmosphere in Clover Grove was anything but normal. Word of Chef Anthony's attack had spread through the town like wildfire, and everyone was on edge. Customers came into the bakery with anxious expressions, their usual cheerful chatter replaced by hushed whispers about the ongoing investigation. Even the sunniest faces now carried a shadow of fear.

Harper noticed the change immediately. The usual warmth that filled her bakery had been replaced by something more somber, as if the very walls had absorbed the town's collective anxiety. The comforting scent of baking bread couldn't completely mask the tension that hung in the air, a palpable unease that seeped into every corner of Clover Grove.

She did her best to stay focused on her work, but her thoughts kept drifting back to the mystery at hand. Rachel continued her research, digging through old records and recipe books in search of clues, while Ethan followed up on leads, trying to piece together what had happened to Chef Anthony. Harper was grateful for their help, but the slow progress gnawed at her. Every day that passed without answers felt like a day closer to something worse.

But despite their efforts, progress was slow, and the tension in the town only grew. Harper could feel it in the air—like the quiet before a storm, when everything is poised on the edge of something big and terrible. She found herself jumping at small noises, her mind always half-listening for the sound of footsteps outside the bakery, or the creak of a door that shouldn't be opening.

One afternoon, as Harper was finishing up a batch of sourdough loaves, the bell above the door jingled, and she looked up to see Amelia Thornton stepping inside. Amelia was a tall, slender woman with long, dark hair and striking blue eyes that always seemed to be watching, calculating. She moved with a grace that was almost feline, her every step measured and deliberate. Amelia had been a close friend of Chef Anthony's, often helping him out at the restaurant when he needed an extra pair of hands.

"Amelia," Harper greeted, her voice tinged with surprise. She hadn't seen Amelia much since the attack, and the woman's sudden appearance put her on edge. "I didn't expect to see you today."

Amelia offered a small, tight-lipped smile as she approached the counter. There was a guardedness in her expression, as if she were holding something back. "I've been keeping to myself lately. Too much going on, you know?"

Harper nodded, understanding the sentiment all too well. "I'm glad you stopped by. How are you holding up?"

Amelia sighed, her expression turning somber. The shift was subtle, but Harper noticed the way Amelia's shoulders slumped slightly, the way her gaze flicked away as if to hide something. "It's been tough. Anthony's like family to me, and seeing him like this... it's hard. But I've been thinking a lot about what happened, and I wanted to talk to you."

Harper's interest piqued, but she also felt a prickle of unease. There was something about the way Amelia spoke, the way she carefully chose her words, that set off warning bells in Harper's mind. "What about?" she asked, keeping her tone neutral.

Amelia hesitated, glancing around the empty bakery as if checking to make sure they were alone. She leaned in slightly, lowering her voice. "It's about Anthony—what he was working on before the attack. He was obsessed with finding something, a recipe or an ingredient, I'm not sure. But he kept saying it was the key to everything."

Harper's heart skipped a beat. There it was again—that sense of something larger, something just out of reach, that had been hovering on the edges of her awareness since this all began. "The key to what?"

"I don't know," Amelia admitted, her voice barely above a whisper. There was a tightness around her eyes, a tension that hadn't been there before. "But whatever it was, it consumed him. He was always at the restaurant, staying late, poring over old books and notes. He barely slept, barely ate. I tried to get him to talk about it, but he just kept saying that he was close, that he couldn't stop now."

Harper felt a chill run down her spine. The image of Chef Anthony, usually so full of life, hunched over dusty books in the middle of the night, his eyes red-rimmed from lack of sleep, sent a shiver through her. This wasn't the man she knew—this was someone who had been driven to the edge by something, or someone. "Do you think it had something to do with the MacLeod Starter?"

Amelia's eyes flickered with uncertainty. She seemed to consider her answer carefully, her gaze never quite meeting Harper's. "It's possible. He mentioned your name a few times, said something about the starter being special, unique. But he wouldn't tell me more than that. It was like he was afraid to say too much."

Harper's mind raced with possibilities. If Chef Anthony had been onto something—something connected to her family's starter—then whoever had attacked him might still be after it. And if Anthony had been afraid to talk about it, that suggested there was more at play than just a simple recipe. The implications were unsettling, to say the least.

"Thank you for telling me this," Harper said, her voice filled with sincerity. Despite the unease that had settled in her stomach, she was grateful for Amelia's honesty. "It means a lot."

Amelia nodded, her expression serious. She seemed to hesitate for a moment, as if debating whether to say more, but then she pressed her lips together and shook her head. "Just be careful, Harper. Whatever Anthony was involved in, it's dangerous. And I have a feeling it's far from over."

As Amelia left the bakery, Harper felt a knot of anxiety tighten in her chest. The more she learned about Chef Anthony's obsession, the more she realized just how deep this mystery went. And the more she understood that the danger was growing closer with each passing day.

The rest of the day passed slowly, each hour dragging as Harper tried to keep her mind focused on the tasks at hand. She kneaded dough, shaped loaves, and greeted customers with a smile that felt increasingly forced. Every time the bell above the door jingled, her heart skipped a beat, half-expecting something—or someone—unexpected to walk in.

By the time she closed up shop for the evening, Harper was exhausted, both physically and mentally. She locked the doors, turned off the lights, and headed upstairs to her apartment above the bakery. The stairs creaked under her weight, the sound echoing in the quiet building, and for a moment, she paused, listening to the silence around her. It was too quiet, too still, and the feeling of being watched that had plagued her the past few days crept back in.

Harper shook her head, trying to push the paranoia away. She was letting her imagination get the best of her. But as she reached the top of the stairs and unlocked her apartment door, the feeling of unease only grew stronger. She hesitated before entering, her hand hovering over the doorknob. Something felt off, though she couldn't quite place it.

Slowly, Harper pushed the door open and stepped inside. The apartment was dark, the only light coming from the faint glow of the streetlamps outside her window. She reached for the light switch, flipping it on with a click. The warm, familiar glow filled the room, but the sense of unease didn't dissipate. If anything, it intensified.

Harper's eyes scanned the room, searching for anything out of place. Everything seemed normal—the kitchen was tidy, her books neatly stacked on the coffee table, her favorite blanket draped over the arm of the couch. But the feeling of being watched, of something lurking just out of sight, was impossible to ignore.

She took a deep breath, trying to calm her racing heart. Maybe she was just tired, worn out from the stress of the past few days. But even as she told herself that, she couldn't shake the feeling that something wasn't right.

Harper moved to the kitchen, her footsteps slow and deliberate. She reached for a glass and filled it with water, taking a long drink in an attempt to steady her nerves. The cool liquid did little to calm her, and she set the glass down on the counter with a shaky hand.

As she turned to leave the kitchen, her eyes caught on something small and out of place—something she hadn't noticed before. A piece of paper, folded neatly, sat on the edge of the counter, half-hidden under a dish towel. Harper's heart skipped a beat as she reached for it, her fingers trembling slightly as she unfolded the note.

The handwriting was unfamiliar, scrawled in a hurried, almost frantic style. Harper's eyes widened as she read the words:

"Stop digging. You don't know what you're getting into. Walk away before it's too late."

Harper's breath caught in her throat, her pulse racing. Someone had been in her apartment. Someone had left this note—someone who didn't want her to uncover the truth. The realization hit her like a punch to the gut, and she stumbled back, her hand gripping the edge of the counter to steady herself.

For a moment, Harper just stood there, staring at the note in her hand, her mind racing. Who had left this? And how had they gotten into her apartment without her knowing? The implications were terrifying. If they had access to her apartment, what else did they know? How closely were they watching her?

Panic threatened to overwhelm her, but Harper forced herself to take a deep breath, to think clearly. She couldn't afford to fall apart now—not when things were escalating so quickly. She needed to be smart, to stay one step ahead.

Her first instinct was to call Ethan, to tell him about the note and ask for his help. But even as she reached for her phone, she hesitated. What if the person who left the note was watching her right now? What if they were listening in on her calls? The thought sent a chill down her spine, and she quickly put the phone back down.

Instead, Harper carefully folded the note and tucked it into her pocket. She needed to be cautious, to play this carefully. If whoever was behind this thought they had scared her off, they might let their guard down. And that could give her the advantage she needed.

But she couldn't do this alone. She needed to talk to Ethan, to Rachel—to anyone who could help her figure out what was going on. And she needed to do it in a way that wouldn't tip off whoever was watching her.

Harper took a deep breath and forced herself to think logically. She couldn't stay in her apartment—it was too vulnerable, too exposed. She needed to get out, to find somewhere safe where she could regroup and plan her next move.

She grabbed her coat and slipped out of the apartment, moving quickly but quietly down the stairs. The cool night air hit her as she stepped outside, and she glanced around, half-expecting to see someone lurking in the shadows. But the street was empty, the town quiet under the blanket of night.

Harper started walking, her steps brisk as she made her way toward the one place she knew she could find help—the library. Rachel would still be there, buried in her research, and together they could figure out what to do next.

As she walked, Harper couldn't shake the feeling that she was being followed. Every rustle of leaves, every distant footstep, made her heart race. She kept her head down, her pace quickening as she neared the library.

When she finally reached the old stone building, Harper breathed a sigh of relief. The warm glow of the lights inside was a welcome sight, a beacon of safety in the midst of the dark. She pushed open the heavy wooden door and stepped inside, the familiar scent of old books and polished wood wrapping around her like a comforting embrace.

"Rachel?" Harper called out, her voice echoing slightly in the quiet space.

Rachel appeared from one of the aisles, a stack of books in her arms. Her brow furrowed with concern as she took in Harper's disheveled appearance. "Harper, what's wrong? You look like you've seen a ghost."

Harper swallowed hard, her hands trembling as she pulled the note from her pocket and handed it to Rachel. "I found this in my apartment. Someone's been watching me, Rachel. They know what we're doing."

Rachel's eyes widened as she read the note, her face paling. "This is serious, Harper. We need to tell Ethan right away."

"I know," Harper said, her voice trembling slightly. "But I'm scared, Rachel. If they can get into my apartment, what else can they do? What if they're watching us right now?"

Rachel placed a comforting hand on Harper's shoulder, her expression determined. "We'll figure this out, Harper. You're not alone in this."

The two women stood in the dimly lit library, the weight of the situation pressing down on them. But even in the face of fear, Harper felt a glimmer of hope. She had allies, people she could trust, and together they would find a way to unravel the mystery that had ensnared Clover Grove.

But as they began to plan their next steps, Harper couldn't shake the feeling that they were running out of time. The danger was growing closer, and whoever was behind this was getting more desperate. They needed to act quickly, before it was too late.

Chapter 9: A Recipe for Danger

That evening, after the bakery had closed and the last of the customers had gone home, Harper sat down with a notebook, determined to piece together everything she had learned so far. The kitchen, usually a place of warmth and comfort, now felt like a war room, the tension palpable as she stared at the scattered notes before her. The only sound was the soft ticking of the clock on the wall, each tick a reminder of how little time they had to unravel the mystery.

She flipped through her notes, her pen tapping rhythmically against the table as she tried to connect the dots. The pieces of the puzzle were there, scattered like breadcrumbs, but no matter how she arranged them, they refused to form a coherent picture. She wrote down the key points: Chef Anthony's obsession with the MacLeod Starter, the old recipe book Rachel had found, the strange note about the yeast, and Amelia's cryptic warning. But each point felt like a riddle, leading to more questions than answers.

Chef Anthony's behavior before the attack had been erratic, his fixation on the starter growing into something almost manic. Harper couldn't shake the image of him, hunched over old books late at night, searching for something he couldn't quite grasp. What had he found—or what had he been close to finding—that had made him a target?

As she sat there, lost in thought, her phone buzzed with a message. The sudden noise startled her, pulling her out of her reverie. It was from Rachel.

"Harper, I've found something new. Meet me at the bakery tomorrow morning."

The message was brief, but it carried a weight of urgency that made Harper's heart race. Rachel had been tirelessly digging through old records, chasing leads that seemed to grow colder by the day. If she had found something new, it could be the breakthrough they desperately needed.

Harper quickly replied, agreeing to meet her friend. The anticipation of what Rachel had found filled her with a renewed sense of purpose, a flicker of hope in the midst of the uncertainty that had been suffocating her.

She tried to get some sleep that night, but her mind refused to quiet. Images of old recipe books, cryptic notes, and the worried faces of her friends danced in her thoughts. She tossed and turned, the weight of the mystery pressing down on her chest, until she finally drifted into a restless sleep.

The next morning, Harper arrived at the bakery early, her mind still buzzing with the remnants of the night's turmoil. The sky was just beginning to lighten, the first rays of dawn casting a soft glow over the town. She unlocked the door and stepped inside, the familiar scent of yeast and flour greeting her like an old friend.

She busied herself with preparations for the day, her hands moving on autopilot as she arranged loaves of bread and pastries on the shelves. But her mind was elsewhere, fixated on the conversation she was about to have with Rachel.

Not long after, the bell above the door jingled, and Harper looked up to see Rachel entering, a stack of papers and books in tow. She looked both exhausted and exhilarated, her eyes gleaming with excitement as she spread out her findings on one of the tables.

"Harper, you're not going to believe what I found," Rachel said, her voice hushed with urgency. There was a certain fervor in her tone, a spark that suggested she had uncovered something truly significant.

"What is it?" Harper asked, moving to stand beside her, her heart pounding with anticipation.

Rachel pointed to an old, leather-bound journal lying open on the table. The cover was worn and cracked, the leather softened by years of use. The pages were yellowed with age, the handwriting elegant but faded, a relic of another time.

"This journal belonged to one of your ancestors—Elspeth MacLeod," Rachel explained, her voice filled with awe. "She was a healer and a baker, known for her remedies and her bread. But what's interesting is this."

She flipped to a page near the middle of the journal, where a recipe for sourdough bread was written in neat script. The ingredients were simple—flour, water, salt, and sourdough starter—but there was a note scribbled in the margin, written in a different hand, as if it had been added later.

"The yeast is the key. Guard it well, for it holds the power to heal and to harm."

Harper's breath caught in her throat as she read the words. They were simple, yet they carried a weight that made her heart pound in her chest. "What does that mean?"

"I think it means that the MacLeod Starter is more than just a recipe," Rachel said, her voice trembling with the gravity of the discovery. "It's something special, something powerful. And if Chef Anthony was trying to recreate it, or if he thought it could make his bread more valuable, someone else might have wanted it too."

Harper felt a chill run down her spine. The idea that her family's starter could be at the center of something so dangerous was both terrifying and surreal. It was as if she had stumbled into a storybook, one where the relics of the past held mystical powers that could change the fate of those who wielded them. But this was no story—this was her life, her family's legacy, and it was quickly becoming a dangerous burden.

"So, you think someone might have attacked him to steal the secret? To get their hands on the starter?" Harper asked, her voice barely above a whisper.

"It's possible," Rachel said. "And if that's the case, then whoever did this might still be looking for it." She paused, her brow furrowing as she considered the implications. "But it's more than just the starter itself, Harper. It's the knowledge, the understanding of how to use it. Your ancestor, Elspeth, wasn't just a baker—she was a healer. She knew how to use the yeast not just to make bread, but for other purposes. If someone figured that out..."

Harper's mind raced as she processed the information. The idea that her family's starter could be at the center of something so dangerous was both terrifying and surreal. But it also made her more determined than ever to protect it.

"We need to be careful," Harper said, her voice steady despite the turmoil inside. The thought of someone using the starter for harm sent a wave of nausea through her. "If someone's willing to hurt Chef Anthony over this, they could come after us next."

Rachel nodded, her expression serious. "Agreed. But we're not backing down. We're going to figure this out, Harper. Together."

As they continued to discuss the possibilities, Harper couldn't shake the feeling that they were on the brink of something big—something that could change everything they thought they knew about Clover Grove and the secrets it held. The stakes had never been higher, and the danger felt more immediate, more personal, than ever before.

Harper's mind flashed back to the note she had found in her apartment, the words scrawled in that frantic hand. "Stop digging. You don't know what you're getting into. Walk away before it's too late." Someone had gone to great lengths to warn her off, to scare her into abandoning the search. But now, more than ever, Harper knew she couldn't walk away. There was too much at stake—her family's legacy, Chef Anthony's life, and perhaps even the safety of Clover Grove itself.

As the morning wore on, the bakery began to fill with customers, the usual bustle of activity returning as the town tried to go about its daily life. But even as Harper served up loaves of bread and pastries, her mind was far from the mundane tasks of running a bakery. She was consumed by the questions swirling in her mind, the pieces of the puzzle that still didn't fit.

She thought about her ancestor, Elspeth MacLeod, a woman who had lived centuries before, yet whose actions were now casting long shadows over the present. What had Elspeth known that was so important? What had she guarded so carefully that even now, it was worth killing for?

KNEADING THE TRUTH

Harper's thoughts were interrupted by the sound of the bell above the door jingling. She looked up to see Detective Ethan Callahan stepping inside, his expression as serious as ever. He approached the counter, his eyes scanning the bakery with a careful, practiced gaze.

"Morning, Harper," Ethan said, his tone neutral, though Harper could sense the tension beneath his calm exterior.

"Morning, Ethan," Harper replied, her voice steadier than she felt. "What brings you by?"

"I wanted to check in, see how you're holding up," Ethan said, though Harper knew there was more to it than that. He was here for a reason, and she had a feeling it had something to do with the investigation.

Harper glanced at Rachel, who gave her a subtle nod, encouraging her to share what they had discovered. Taking a deep breath, Harper decided to trust Ethan with the information.

"We found something," Harper said, lowering her voice as she gestured for Ethan to follow her to a quieter corner of the bakery. "Rachel found an old journal, one that belonged to my ancestor, Elspeth MacLeod. There's a note in it—something about the yeast being the key, and how it holds the power to heal and harm."

Ethan's eyes narrowed, his expression growing more intense. "And you think that's connected to what happened to Chef Anthony?"

"It's possible," Rachel chimed in, her voice steady as she explained. "Elspeth was a healer, but she was also a baker. The MacLeod Starter wasn't just used to make bread—it was part of her remedies, part of something bigger. If Chef Anthony figured that out, or if he was close to discovering it, someone might have wanted to stop him."

Ethan listened carefully, his expression unreadable as he processed the information. "This could be a significant lead," he said finally. "But it also means we're dealing with something more complicated than we initially thought."

Harper nodded, her heart pounding in her chest. "What do we do now?"

"We need to be vigilant," Ethan said, his tone firm. "If someone is after this starter, they might come after you next, Harper. We need to make sure you're safe."

The words sent a chill through Harper, but she knew Ethan was right. The danger was real, and it was growing. But she also knew that she couldn't back down—not when they were so close to uncovering the truth.

"I'll be careful," Harper promised, though the weight of the situation was pressing down on her more heavily than ever. "But we can't stop now. We're too close."

Ethan's expression softened slightly, a flicker of admiration in his eyes. "Just promise me you won't take any unnecessary risks."

Harper managed a small smile, though it didn't reach her eyes. "I promise."

As Ethan left the bakery, Harper turned back to Rachel, who was already poring over the journal again, her brow furrowed in concentration.

"We're going to find out what's really going on," Harper said, her voice filled with determination. "And we're going to stop whoever's behind this."

KNEADING THE TRUTH

Rachel looked up, her eyes filled with the same resolve. "We will, Harper. Together."

As the day wore on, Harper found herself reflecting on how much had changed in such a short time. What had started as a simple mystery—a baker attacked, a family recipe at the center—had spiraled into something much more complex, much more dangerous. But it had also brought her closer to the people around her—to Rachel, to Ethan, to the community of Clover Grove. They were all connected, bound together by the threads of the past and the challenges of the present.

And as the sun began to set, casting long shadows across the town, Harper knew that they were on the verge of a breakthrough. The secrets that had been buried for centuries were starting to surface, and with them, the truth about the MacLeod Starter, about Chef Anthony, and about the forces that had been set in motion long before any of them were born.

But there was still much they didn't know, and the path ahead was fraught with danger. Harper could feel it in her bones—the sense that something was coming, something that would test them all in ways they couldn't yet imagine.

As she closed up the bakery that evening, Harper took one last look at the journal lying on the counter, its pages filled with the words of a woman who had lived centuries ago, yet whose influence was still felt today. Elspeth MacLeod had understood the power she held, and she had guarded it fiercely, knowing that it was both a gift and a burden.

Now, that burden had passed to Harper. And she was ready to carry it, no matter what lay ahead.

Chapter 10: The Rising Tension

The days that followed were a whirlwind of activity. Harper, Rachel, and Ethan continued their investigation, each following different leads and piecing together the clues that pointed to a larger, more sinister plot. Despite their best efforts, progress was slow, and the tension in Clover Grove only grew, spreading through the town like a creeping fog that refused to lift.

Harper threw herself into her work at the bakery, using the familiar routines to keep her mind occupied. She kneaded dough with more force than necessary, shaped loaves with meticulous precision, and focused on the rhythm of baking, trying to drown out the anxiety that gnawed at her. But no matter how hard she tried to focus, the shadow of the mystery loomed over her, casting a pall over even the simplest of tasks.

The bakery was quieter than usual, the customers subdued as they whispered about the ongoing investigation. Harper could feel their eyes on her, their curiosity mingling with concern as they tried to make sense of what was happening in their small, close-knit community. The once warm and lively atmosphere had shifted, replaced by an undercurrent of fear that no one could quite name but everyone felt.

As she served customers, Harper caught snippets of conversation—speculation about who could be behind the attack on Chef Anthony, rumors about strange goings-on in town, and hushed worries about what might happen next. The uncertainty was eating away at Clover Grove, and Harper could see it in the tense smiles and nervous glances exchanged by the townspeople. It was as if the entire town was holding its breath, waiting for something to happen.

One afternoon, as Harper was preparing a new batch of sourdough loaves, the bell above the door jingled, and she looked up to see Ethan stepping inside. His expression was serious, his usual easy-going demeanor replaced by a tension that mirrored her own. There was a heaviness in his eyes, a sign that the investigation was taking its toll on him as well.

"Harper," Ethan greeted, his voice low and urgent. "We need to talk."

Harper set down the dough she had been working on and wiped her hands on a towel, her heart pounding with anticipation. She had grown accustomed to Ethan's visits, but there was something different about him today—something that told her this wasn't just a routine check-in. "What's going on?" she asked, her voice steady despite the unease that was beginning to coil in her stomach.

Ethan leaned against the counter, his eyes searching hers for a moment before he spoke. "We've got a lead—a potential witness who might have seen something the night Chef Anthony was attacked. But there's a catch."

Harper frowned, her mind racing. They had been grasping at straws for days, hoping for a breakthrough. Now that they finally had one, she wasn't sure whether to feel relieved or wary. "What kind of catch?" she asked, her voice tinged with apprehension.

"The witness is a recluse, lives on the outskirts of town," Ethan explained, his tone cautious. "She's not exactly... cooperative. But she's agreed to talk to us, on one condition."

Harper's curiosity piqued, though a sense of foreboding quickly followed. In a situation like this, conditions were rarely good news. "What condition?"

"She wants to meet with you," Ethan said, his gaze locking onto hers. "Alone."

Harper's stomach twisted with a mix of fear and curiosity. The request was strange, and it set off alarm bells in her mind. "Why me?" she asked, trying to keep her voice even.

"I'm not sure," Ethan admitted, his expression serious. "But she was adamant. She said she wouldn't talk to anyone else."

Harper considered the request, her mind racing with possibilities. If this witness had information that could help them solve the mystery, it was worth the risk. But the idea of going alone, without Ethan or Rachel by her side, filled her with a sense of unease. There was something about the situation that didn't sit right with her, but she couldn't ignore the possibility that this could be the break they needed.

"I'll do it," Harper said, her voice steady despite the anxiety gnawing at her insides. She wasn't about to let fear hold her back, not when they were so close to uncovering the truth. "But I want you close by, just in case."

Ethan's expression softened with relief, though the tension in his shoulders remained. "I wouldn't let you go alone. We'll keep this quiet, so no one else finds out. If this witness knows something, we need to hear it."

Harper nodded, appreciating his support more than she could say. She had grown to trust Ethan implicitly, and knowing he would be nearby gave her the strength to face whatever lay ahead. As they made plans to meet with the witness, Harper couldn't shake the feeling that they were getting closer to the truth. But with that truth came increased danger—both for herself and those she cared about.

The next morning, Harper prepared herself for the meeting with the witness. She dressed simply, in comfortable clothes that wouldn't hinder her movement if things went south. Her mind buzzed with a mixture of anticipation and dread as she imagined what this reclusive witness might know—and what they might demand in return for that knowledge.

As she prepared to leave, Rachel stopped by the bakery, her eyes filled with concern. "Are you sure about this, Harper?" she asked, her voice laced with worry. "It sounds risky."

"I'm sure," Harper replied, though her heart was pounding in her chest. "We need to know what this witness saw. It could be the key to everything."

Rachel nodded, though she didn't look entirely convinced. "Just be careful. I don't like the idea of you going alone."

"Ethan will be close by," Harper reassured her. "And I'll be on my guard. Don't worry—I'll be fine."

Rachel sighed, but she didn't press the issue further. She knew Harper well enough to understand that once her mind was made up, there was no changing it. "Just promise me you'll call if anything feels off."

"I promise," Harper said, giving Rachel a reassuring smile.

With a final nod, Rachel left the bakery, leaving Harper alone with her thoughts. She took a deep breath, trying to steady her nerves, then grabbed her coat and headed out the door.

The drive to the outskirts of town was a quiet one, the road winding through dense woods that seemed to close in around her the farther she went. The trees, tall and ancient, loomed overhead, their branches casting long shadows across the road. The sense of isolation grew with each passing mile, and by the time Harper reached the small, weathered cabin where the witness lived, she felt as though she had entered another world entirely—one far removed from the safety of Clover Grove.

Ethan was already there, waiting in his car just down the road from the cabin. He gave her a nod as she pulled up, his expression one of quiet determination. "I'll be right here," he said as she stepped out of her car. "If anything happens, I'm coming in."

"Got it," Harper replied, her voice steadier than she felt. She knew Ethan wouldn't let anything happen to her, but the weight of what she was about to do pressed heavily on her shoulders.

The cabin was small and unassuming, its wooden walls weathered by time and the elements. There was no sign of life outside—no car in the driveway, no lights in the windows. It looked like the kind of place where secrets went to die, hidden away from the prying eyes of the world.

Harper approached the front door, her heart pounding in her chest. She hesitated for a moment, her hand hovering over the doorknob as she gathered her courage. Then, with a deep breath, she knocked.

There was a long, tense silence, and for a moment, Harper wondered if she had made a mistake—if the witness had changed their mind or if this had all been a wild goose chase. But just as she was about to turn away, the door creaked open, revealing a woman standing in the shadows.

The woman was older, her hair silver and tied back in a loose bun. Her eyes, sharp and penetrating, studied Harper for a long moment before she stepped aside and gestured for her to enter.

"You're Harper MacLeod," the woman said, her voice rough from disuse. It wasn't a question—it was a statement of fact.

"I am," Harper replied, stepping inside the cabin. The air was thick with the scent of wood smoke and herbs, and the dim light made it difficult to see much of the interior. "And you're the one who saw what happened to Chef Anthony?"

The woman nodded, closing the door behind her. "I am. But I'll tell you right now, what I saw isn't going to be easy to hear."

Harper's heart skipped a beat. "Tell me anyway."

The woman led her to a small table in the center of the room, where two chairs were set up. She motioned for Harper to sit, then took the other chair herself. For a moment, the two women sat in silence, the tension thick in the air between them.

Finally, the woman spoke. "What I saw that night wasn't just an attack. It was a ritual—a ritual meant to take something from Chef Anthony, something important."

Harper felt a chill run down her spine. "A ritual?"

The woman nodded, her expression grim. "It wasn't just about hurting him. It was about taking his knowledge, his connection to the MacLeod Starter. They wanted what he knew, and they were willing to do whatever it took to get it."

Harper's mind raced as she tried to process what the woman was saying. A ritual? The idea seemed almost too strange to be true, but something in the woman's eyes told Harper she was telling the truth.

"Who were they?" Harper asked, her voice trembling slightly.

"I don't know," the woman admitted, her eyes narrowing. "They wore masks, cloaks—like something out of an old story. But I could tell they were dangerous. They knew what they were doing, and they weren't going to stop until they got what they wanted."

Harper's stomach churned with a mix of fear and anger. "And what did they want?"

"They wanted the power of the MacLeod Starter," the woman said, her voice barely above a whisper. "They believe it holds the key to something ancient, something powerful. And they'll stop at nothing to get it."

The words hung in the air, heavy with implication. Harper's mind raced as she tried to piece together what the woman was saying. The power of the starter—the ritual, the masked figures—it all sounded like something out of a nightmare. But deep down, Harper knew there was truth in it.

"What do I do?" Harper asked, her voice trembling.

The woman's eyes softened slightly, her gaze filled with a strange mixture of pity and respect. "You protect the starter, Harper. You protect it with everything you have, because if they get their hands on it, there's no telling what they'll do."

Harper nodded, her resolve hardening. She had always known the starter was important, but now she understood just how much was at stake. She couldn't let it fall into the wrong hands—no matter what it took.

The woman stood, signaling that the conversation was over. "Be careful, Harper. They're watching you. They know who you are."

Harper's blood ran cold at the woman's words, but she forced herself to nod. "Thank you," she said, her voice barely above a whisper.

The woman gave her a curt nod, then turned and opened the door, signaling for Harper to leave. Without another word, Harper stepped outside, the cold air hitting her like a slap to the face. She walked quickly back to her car, her mind spinning with what she had just learned.

Ethan was waiting, his eyes searching hers as she approached. "What did she say?"

Harper climbed into the passenger seat, her hands shaking. "It was more than just an attack," she said, her voice hollow. "It was a ritual. They wanted to take something from him—something connected to the starter."

Ethan's expression darkened, and he started the car, pulling away from the cabin. "We need to talk to Rachel," he said, his tone grim. "This is bigger than we thought."

As they drove back to town, Harper couldn't shake the feeling of eyes on her, watching her every move. The weight of the mystery was pressing down on her more heavily than ever, but now it was tinged with fear—a fear that had settled deep in her bones.

She knew now that they were dealing with something ancient, something powerful—and something that wouldn't stop until it got what it wanted. The stakes were higher than ever, and the danger was all too real.

But Harper also knew she couldn't back down. Not now. Not when they were so close to uncovering the truth.

As they pulled up in front of the bakery, Harper took a deep breath, her mind racing with everything that had happened. She had a feeling that things were about to get much worse before they got better, but she was ready to face whatever came next.

With a final glance at Ethan, Harper stepped out of the car, determination in her eyes. She was going to protect the MacLeod Starter—no matter what it took.

Chapter 11: The Hidden Key

The next morning, Harper and Ethan drove to the outskirts of Clover Grove, where the town gave way to rolling hills and dense forests. The landscape was a stark contrast to the bustling town center, the quiet serenity of nature creating an eerie calm. It was as if the world itself was holding its breath, waiting for something to happen.

The witness, a woman named Agnes Reed, lived in a small, isolated cabin, far from the hustle and bustle of town life. She was known for her eccentricities, and few in Clover Grove had ever ventured out to her home. The locals whispered about her—stories of her odd behavior, her supposed clairvoyance, and her connection to the old ways that had long since faded from the town's collective memory. But today, Agnes Reed was their only lead.

As they approached the cabin, Harper's anxiety grew. The trees closed in around them, casting long shadows across the narrow dirt road. The air was thick with the scent of pine and earth, and the silence was almost oppressive. It was the kind of quiet that made every sound, every rustle of leaves, feel amplified, and Harper's heartbeat seemed to echo in her ears.

Ethan pulled the car to a stop a short distance from the cabin, his expression tense. He turned off the engine, and the sudden silence was deafening. "Are you sure you're okay with this?" he asked, his voice a low rumble that seemed to blend with the quiet around them.

Harper nodded, though her heart was pounding in her chest. The cabin, with its weathered wooden walls and a thin wisp of smoke curling from the chimney, looked like something out of a forgotten past. It exuded a sense of otherworldliness that made Harper feel both drawn to and wary of what lay inside. "I'm okay. Let's do this."

Ethan gave her a reassuring smile, though the worry in his eyes was clear. "I'll be right here. If anything feels off, you come straight back."

Harper nodded again, taking a deep breath to steady herself before stepping out of the car. The forest seemed to close in around her as she walked toward the cabin, the crunch of gravel under her feet the only sound breaking the stillness. She could feel Ethan's gaze on her back, a comforting presence even as she moved farther away from him.

The cabin was small and weathered, its wooden walls gray with age and the weight of countless winters. The windows were dark, their glass panes reflecting the trees that surrounded the cabin like silent sentinels. A thin wisp of smoke curled from the chimney, the only sign of life. Harper hesitated for a moment, glancing back at Ethan one last time. He gave her a small nod of encouragement, and with that, she raised her hand and knocked on the door.

For a long moment, there was no response. Harper was about to knock again when the door creaked open, revealing an elderly woman with sharp, piercing eyes that seemed to see straight through her. Agnes Reed was a slight woman, her gray hair pulled back in a loose bun, and her expression was one of wary curiosity. Her skin was weathered, etched with lines that told stories of a long life lived in solitude.

"You must be Harper MacLeod," Agnes said, her voice raspy but clear. There was a sharpness to her tone, as if she had been expecting this meeting for a long time.

"Yes, ma'am," Harper replied, her voice steady despite the unease that gnawed at her. Standing before Agnes, Harper felt a strange mix of familiarity and apprehension, as if this encounter was something that had been written long before she was born. "Detective Callahan said you wanted to speak with me."

Agnes nodded slowly, her eyes narrowing as she studied Harper. "Come inside, then. But mind your step. The floor's not what it used to be." Her voice was tinged with a hint of wry humor, but her eyes remained serious, almost challenging.

Harper followed Agnes into the cabin, her senses on high alert. The interior was dimly lit, the walls lined with shelves filled with books, jars, and odd trinkets that seemed to defy categorization. The air was thick with the scent of herbs and wood smoke, and the flickering light from the fire in the small hearth cast long, dancing shadows across the room. There was a sense of timelessness here, as if the outside world had no place within these walls.

Agnes motioned for Harper to sit at a small table near the fire, then took a seat across from her. For a moment, neither of them spoke, the only sound the crackling of the fire and the creaking of the old wooden beams. Harper took in her surroundings, her gaze lingering on the strange objects that filled the shelves—dried herbs, animal bones, and what appeared to be a collection of antique keys.

"You're here because of Anthony, aren't you?" Agnes said finally, her eyes never leaving Harper's. There was a weight to her words, as if they carried more than just the question she was asking.

Harper nodded. "Yes. We're trying to find out what happened to him, and Detective Callahan said you might have seen something that night."

Agnes's gaze softened slightly, though her expression remained guarded. "I did see something. But that's not why I wanted to talk to you."

Harper's heart skipped a beat. The room seemed to close in around her, the flickering firelight casting an ominous glow. "Then why did you ask for me?"

Agnes leaned forward, her voice lowering to a conspiratorial whisper. "Because you're a MacLeod. And the key to all of this lies in your family's past."

Harper's breath caught in her throat. "What do you mean?" The words tumbled out before she could stop them, her curiosity now a burning need to know.

Agnes's eyes glittered with a strange intensity, a light that seemed to come from somewhere deep within. "The MacLeod Starter. It's more than just a recipe, more than just yeast. It's a link to something old, something powerful. And there are those who would do anything to get their hands on it."

Harper's mind raced as she tried to process what Agnes was saying. She had always known the starter was special, a family heirloom passed down through generations, but this—this was something else entirely. "But how do you know about the starter? How is it connected to what happened to Chef Anthony?"

Agnes hesitated, her expression pained. She looked away for a moment, as if gathering her thoughts, before turning her piercing gaze back to Harper. "I've lived in Clover Grove my whole life, and I've seen things—things most people wouldn't believe. Your family's starter has always been special, but there's more to it than just the yeast. It's tied to an old legend, one that dates back centuries. Anthony was trying to uncover the truth, but he didn't understand the danger."

Harper's pulse quickened. The room seemed to grow warmer, the fire's heat pressing against her skin. "What kind of danger?"

Agnes's voice dropped to a whisper. "There are those who believe that the starter holds the key to something powerful—something that could change the world, or destroy it. And they'll stop at nothing to get it."

Harper felt a chill run down her spine, despite the heat of the fire. "Who are they?"

Agnes's eyes darkened, the light within them dimming as her expression grew serious. "They call themselves The Alchemists. They've been searching for the key for centuries, and they've finally found it. But they don't understand the true nature of what they seek."

The Alchemists. The name sent a shiver through Harper, the weight of it settling in her chest like a leaden ball. "What do they want with the starter?"

Agnes shook her head, her expression filled with a mixture of sorrow and resolve. "They believe it's the key to immortality, to ultimate power. They've chased myths and legends across the globe, searching for anything that could give them the edge they desire. And now they believe your family's starter is that key."

Harper's mind whirled with questions, but before she could ask more, Agnes leaned back in her chair, her expression weary. "But they're wrong," Agnes continued, her voice tinged with regret. "The power they seek—it's not what they think. It's dangerous, uncontrollable. If they get their hands on it..."

Harper swallowed hard, her throat dry. "How do you know all of this?"

Agnes looked at her with a gaze that seemed to pierce through time itself. "My family was once part of their circle. My ancestors broke away when they realized the true nature of the power they were dealing with. But the knowledge, the secrets—they've been passed down, just as your starter has. I've spent my life watching, waiting, knowing that one day they would come for it."

Harper felt the weight of those words, the gravity of what she was being told. The responsibility that had been passed down to her was far greater than she had ever imagined. "What do I do?"

Agnes's eyes softened slightly, her gaze filled with a strange mixture of pity and respect. "You protect the starter, Harper. You protect it with everything you have, because if they get their hands on it, there's no telling what they'll do."

Harper nodded, her resolve hardening. She had always known the starter was important, but now she understood just how much was at stake. She couldn't let it fall into the wrong hands—no matter what it took. "How do I stop them?"

Agnes leaned forward, her voice barely above a whisper. "There's an old text, hidden in the town's archives. It's written in a language few can read, but it holds the answers you seek.

It will guide you, show you how to protect the starter, how to keep it safe from those who would use it for harm."

Harper's mind raced, but before she could ask more, Agnes stood, signaling that the conversation was over. "I've said enough," Agnes said, her voice tinged with finality. "But know this, Harper MacLeod: the key lies in your hands now. And what you do with it will determine the fate of us all."

Harper's thoughts were a tangled knot of fear, confusion, and determination as she left the cabin and made her way back to the car. The mystery was deeper and more dangerous than she had ever imagined, and the stakes were higher than she had ever anticipated.

Ethan was waiting by the car, his expression filled with concern as he saw Harper's pale face. "What did she say?" he asked, his voice gentle but urgent.

Harper shook her head, trying to make sense of everything she had just learned. "She told me about a group called The Alchemists. They believe the starter is the key to something powerful—something dangerous."

Ethan's expression darkened, his jaw clenching as he processed the information. "We need to talk to Rachel," he said, his voice firm. "If there's a text in the archives that can help us, we need to find it."

Harper nodded, her mind already racing ahead to what needed to be done. The truth was within their reach, but so was the danger. And they had to be ready for whatever came next.

As they drove back to town, the weight of what she had learned settled heavily on Harper's shoulders. The responsibility that had been passed down to her was greater than she had ever imagined, and the danger more real. But one thing was clear: she couldn't turn back now. The truth was within her reach, and she was determined to uncover it—no matter what the cost.

The drive back to Clover Grove was quiet, the tension between them palpable. Harper couldn't stop thinking about the responsibility that now rested on her shoulders. She had always known the starter was special, but now she understood just how significant it was. The future of the town—perhaps even more—depended on her ability to protect it.

As they neared the town, Harper glanced at Ethan. "We need to be careful. If these Alchemists are as dangerous as Agnes says, they're not going to stop until they get what they want."

Ethan nodded, his expression grim. "We'll take every precaution. But we need to act quickly. If there's a text in the archives that can help us, we need to find it before they do."

Harper felt a surge of determination. The stakes had never been higher, but she wasn't about to let fear stop her. She had the support of her friends, the knowledge of her ancestors, and the will to see this through.

As they pulled into Clover Grove, Harper knew that the real fight was just beginning. The Alchemists were out there, and they were closing in. But Harper was ready. She would protect the MacLeod Starter with everything she had, because now she knew—it was the key to something far greater than herself, something that could change the world forever.

Chapter 12: A Sourdough Revelation

Harper returned to the bakery with a heavy heart and a mind buzzing with the revelations Agnes had shared. The idea that her family's starter could be connected to something so ancient and powerful was both thrilling and terrifying. It was as if the world she had always known had suddenly expanded, revealing depths and dangers she had never imagined. But it also made her more determined than ever to protect the starter—and to find out the truth that had been hidden for centuries.

The familiar scents of yeast and flour surrounded her as she stood in the quiet bakery, the only sounds the ticking of the wall clock and the hum of the refrigerator. The early morning light filtered through the windows, casting long shadows across the wooden floor. Harper couldn't help but feel a deep connection to her ancestors, to the generations of MacLeods who had come before her. The starter was more than just a recipe—it was a piece of history, a legacy that had been passed down through the centuries, from mother to daughter, father to son. It was the heart of her family, and now it was in danger.

As she paced the floor of the bakery, her thoughts raced. She knew she needed to be careful, but she also knew that she couldn't do this alone. The weight of the responsibility was too great, the danger too real. She needed help—someone she could trust, someone who understood the gravity of the situation.

And the first person who came to mind was Ethan.

Harper grabbed her phone and quickly dialed his number. Her fingers trembled slightly as she pressed the buttons, the reality of what she was about to do sinking in. After a few rings, Ethan answered, his voice steady and reassuring.

"Harper, what's going on?" he asked, his tone instantly alert, sensing the urgency in her voice.

"I need to talk to you," Harper said, her voice urgent. "It's about the starter. I think I know what's going on, but I need your help."

There was a brief pause on the other end of the line before Ethan replied, "Alright. I'll be there in a few minutes."

As she waited for Ethan to arrive, Harper tried to calm her racing heart. She began to prepare a new batch of dough, her hands moving automatically as she thought about what she would say. The process of mixing the ingredients, feeling the dough come together under her fingers, usually brought her a sense of peace. But today, her mind was too full, the weight of the revelations pressing down on her.

The dough was soft and pliable under her fingers, a reminder of the generations of bakers who had come before her. She thought of her grandmother, Fiona, who had taught her the secrets of the starter, passing down the knowledge that had been handed to her by her own mother. Harper had always thought of the starter as a symbol of family, of tradition, but now she realized it was so much more. It was a link to the past, a key to a mystery that had been hidden for centuries.

When Ethan arrived, Harper wasted no time in explaining what she had learned from Agnes. She told him about the legend, the Alchemists, and the connection to the MacLeod

Starter. The words spilled out of her in a rush, as if saying them aloud could somehow make them more real, more manageable.

Ethan listened intently, his expression growing more serious with each passing moment. He didn't interrupt, didn't question her, just let her talk until she had said everything that needed to be said. When Harper finished, he let out a slow breath, his eyes locked on hers.

"This is bigger than I thought," Ethan said, his voice filled with concern. "If what Agnes said is true, then we're dealing with something that goes way beyond a simple attack. We need to be careful, Harper. These people—The Alchemists—they sound dangerous."

"I know," Harper replied, her voice steady despite the turmoil inside. The reality of the situation was sinking in, the fear and the responsibility mixing together in a way that made her feel both vulnerable and determined. "But we can't just ignore this. We need to find out what they're after, and why they think the starter is the key."

Ethan nodded, his expression thoughtful as he weighed their options. "Agreed. But we need to do this the right way. I'll look into The Alchemists, see what I can find out. In the meantime, you should keep a low profile. Don't let anyone know what you've learned—especially not about the starter."

Harper nodded, feeling a surge of gratitude for Ethan's support. His calm, measured approach was exactly what she needed right now. "I will. And Ethan—thank you. For believing me."

Ethan's expression softened, and he gave her a small smile, the kind that always made her feel like everything was going to be okay, even when it wasn't. "I always believe you, Harper. We're in this together."

As Ethan left the bakery, Harper felt a renewed sense of purpose. The mystery was far from over, but with Ethan by her side, she felt stronger—more capable of facing whatever challenges lay ahead. The bakery, which had always been her sanctuary, now felt like the center of something much larger, a battleground where the past and the present were colliding.

Harper decided to take a moment to reflect on everything she had learned. She walked over to the table where she kept the starter, a simple glass jar filled with the bubbling mixture that held so much history, so much power. She gently placed her hand on the jar, feeling the warmth of the dough inside, the life that was so much a part of her family's legacy.

She remembered the stories her grandmother had told her, tales of the MacLeod ancestors who had fled Scotland, bringing the starter with them across the ocean to America. The starter had survived wars, famine, and countless hardships, a constant in a world that was always changing. It was a symbol of resilience, of the strength of the MacLeod line, and now it was up to Harper to protect it.

But what did The Alchemists want with it? The question gnawed at her, a puzzle she couldn't quite piece together. The idea that the starter could hold the key to something as powerful as immortality or ultimate power seemed like the stuff of fairy tales, and yet, everything she had learned suggested there was truth to it.

The Alchemists had been searching for centuries, following clues, chasing legends, and now they were here, in Clover Grove, knocking on Harper's door. The thought made her

KNEADING THE TRUTH 99

stomach turn. What if they were watching her right now, waiting for the right moment to strike? The idea sent a shiver down her spine, but she pushed the fear aside. She couldn't afford to be afraid—not now.

Determined to find out more, Harper decided to dig deeper into her family's history. She needed to understand the connection between the starter and the legends Agnes had spoken of. There had to be something in the old family records, something that could give her a clue.

She went upstairs to her small apartment above the bakery, where she kept a collection of old journals and letters that had been passed down through the generations. They were kept in a sturdy wooden chest, one of the few things she had inherited from her grandmother. Harper knelt beside the chest and carefully opened it, the scent of aged paper and leather filling the room.

The journals were worn, their pages yellowed with age, but they were a treasure trove of information, a window into the lives of her ancestors. Harper flipped through the pages, her fingers tracing the elegant script that had been written by hands long gone. There were recipes, notes on the care of the starter, and stories of the MacLeod family's journey from Scotland to America.

As she read, Harper began to piece together the story of the MacLeod Starter. It had been brought to America by her great-great-grandmother, Elspeth MacLeod, who had been a healer and a midwife in her village in Scotland. The starter had been part of her healing practices, used not just for baking bread, but for making poultices and medicines that were said to have extraordinary properties.

Elspeth had been revered in her village, known as much for her wisdom as for her baking. But there had also been whispers, rumors that she possessed knowledge that had been passed down from the old days, from the time of the druids. The villagers had called her a witch, though they had done so with a mix of fear and respect. They knew better than to cross her, for they believed she held the power of life and death in her hands.

Harper's heart pounded as she read Elspeth's words, the story of how she had been forced to flee her village when the rumors had grown too dangerous. She had taken the starter with her, hiding it away from those who would misuse its power. She had written of her fears, of the knowledge she carried, and of the responsibility she felt to protect it.

It was clear now that The Alchemists had been hunting for the starter even then, and that Elspeth had gone to great lengths to keep it hidden. She had passed it down to her daughter, with strict instructions to guard it with her life. The journals were filled with warnings, advice on how to care for the starter, and cryptic references to the power it held.

But there was one journal, smaller than the others, bound in worn leather and tucked away at the bottom of the chest, that caught Harper's eye. It was different from the others, its pages filled not with recipes or stories, but with symbols and codes, written in a hand that was unfamiliar. Harper's breath caught in her throat as she realized what she was holding—a key, perhaps, to unlocking the mystery of the starter.

She carefully opened the journal, her eyes scanning the pages, trying to make sense of the symbols. It was clear that this was no ordinary journal; it was a cipher, a puzzle that needed to be solved. The symbols were intricate, their meanings hidden within layers of history and myth. Harper's pulse quickened as she realized that this might be what The Alchemists were after—a map to the true power of the starter.

But she couldn't decipher it alone. She needed help, and there was only one person she could think of who might be able to crack the code—Rachel.

Harper quickly gathered the journals, carefully wrapping them in a cloth to protect them. She placed the bundle in her bag and hurried back down to the bakery, her mind racing. She grabbed her phone and called Rachel, her heart pounding as she waited for her friend to answer.

"Harper, what's up?" Rachel's voice came through the line, filled with curiosity.

"Rachel, I found something," Harper said, her voice urgent. "It's an old journal, written in some kind of code. I think it's connected to the starter—and to The Alchemists. Can you meet me at the bakery?"

There was a brief pause before Rachel replied, "I'll be there as soon as I can."

Harper hung up the phone, her mind buzzing with anticipation. The pieces of the puzzle were starting to come together, and she was one step closer to uncovering the truth. But with that truth came increased danger, and Harper knew they had to be careful.

As she waited for Rachel to arrive, Harper couldn't help but think about the legacy she was protecting. The MacLeod Starter was more than just a recipe—it was a piece of history, a link to the past, and a key to the future. And now, it was in her hands. The weight of that responsibility settled heavily on her shoulders, but it also filled her with a sense of purpose.

When Rachel arrived, Harper wasted no time in showing her the journal. Together, they pored over the pages, their heads bent close as they tried to make sense of the symbols and codes. It was slow going, the meanings elusive, but Rachel's knowledge of ancient languages and codes proved invaluable.

As they worked, the sun dipped lower in the sky, casting long shadows across the bakery. The air grew cooler, the scent of baking bread mingling with the earthy smell of the old journal. Hours passed, and the outside world seemed to fade away as they became absorbed in their task.

Finally, as the first stars appeared in the night sky, Rachel let out a triumphant cry. "I think I've got it!"

Harper leaned closer, her heart pounding. "What does it say?"

Rachel carefully translated the symbols, her voice steady as she read aloud. "The power of the starter lies not in the yeast itself, but in the knowledge of how to use it. The Alchemists seek immortality, but they do not understand the true nature of the gift. It is not life everlasting, but the ability to heal and to nourish, to bring life where there was none. But in the wrong hands, this power can be twisted, turned to darkness. The key is balance, the harmony between life and death, creation and destruction. The starter is the vessel, but the power lies within the one who wields it."

Harper's breath caught in her throat as the words sank in. The starter wasn't just a recipe—it was a tool, a powerful artifact that could be used for both good and evil. And now, that power was in her hands.

She looked at Rachel, her eyes wide with realization. "We have to protect it. We can't let The Alchemists get their hands on this."

Rachel nodded, her expression serious. "But how? They're already here, already searching. We need to find a way to stop them—before it's too late."

Harper felt a surge of determination. The responsibility that had been passed down to her was greater than she had ever imagined, but she wasn't going to back down. She had the knowledge, the support of her friends, and the will to see this through.

"We'll figure it out," Harper said, her voice filled with resolve. "We'll stop them—no matter what it takes."

As the night deepened and the bakery grew quiet, Harper and Rachel continued their work, their minds focused on the task ahead. The mystery of the MacLeod Starter was far from solved, but they were closer than ever to understanding its true power. And with that understanding came a new sense of purpose—a mission to protect the legacy of the MacLeod family and to ensure that the power of the starter was used for good.

But even as they worked, Harper couldn't shake the feeling that they were running out of time. The Alchemists were closing in, and the stakes had never been higher. The battle for the starter was just beginning, and Harper knew that the outcome would determine the fate of them all.

Chapter 13: The Secrets of Sourdough

The days that followed were filled with a tense anticipation that seemed to permeate every corner of Clover Grove. Harper, Rachel, and Ethan continued their investigation, each following different leads and piecing together the clues that pointed to a larger, more sinister plot. But despite their best efforts, progress was slow, and the tension in Clover Grove only grew, weaving itself into the fabric of the town like an unseen thread pulling everyone closer to the inevitable.

Harper threw herself into her work at the bakery, using the familiar routines to keep her mind occupied. She spent hours kneading dough, the rhythmic motions usually a source of comfort, now tinged with an undercurrent of anxiety. She would stare at the bubbling sourdough starter, wondering how something so seemingly simple could hold the key to a mystery that spanned centuries. But no matter how hard she tried to focus on her work, the shadow of the mystery loomed over her, casting a pall over even the simplest of tasks. The comforting scent of freshly baked bread, once a soothing balm for her soul, now felt like a reminder of the heavy burden she carried.

The bakery was quieter than usual, the customers subdued as they whispered about the ongoing investigation. Harper could feel their eyes on her, their curiosity mingling with concern as they tried to make sense of what was happening in their small, close-knit community. The warmth and camaraderie that usually filled the air were replaced by an uneasy silence, broken only by the occasional nervous laughter or the clink of a coffee cup being set down a little too forcefully.

One afternoon, as Harper was preparing a new batch of sourdough loaves, the bell above the door jingled, and she looked up to see Amelia Thornton stepping inside. Amelia was a tall, slender woman with long, dark hair and striking blue eyes that always seemed to be watching, calculating. There was an air of mystery about her, a sense that she knew more than she let on. She had been a close friend of Chef Anthony's, often helping him out at the restaurant when he needed an extra pair of hands.

"Amelia," Harper greeted, her voice tinged with surprise. Amelia hadn't been around much since the attack on Chef Anthony, and seeing her now stirred a mix of emotions in Harper. "I didn't expect to see you today."

Amelia offered a small, tight-lipped smile as she approached the counter. "I've been keeping to myself lately. Too much going on, you know?" Her voice was calm, but there was a tension in her posture, a tightness around her eyes that suggested she was holding something back.

Harper nodded, understanding the sentiment all too well. The days had been heavy, each one stretching out longer than the last as the weight of unanswered questions bore down on her. "I'm glad you stopped by. How are you holding up?"

Amelia sighed, her expression turning somber. She glanced around the bakery, as if to make sure they were alone before speaking. "It's been tough. Anthony's like family to me, and seeing him like this... it's hard. But I've been thinking a lot about what happened, and I wanted to talk to you."

Harper's interest piqued. Amelia's tone was careful, deliberate, and it put Harper on edge. "What about?"

Amelia hesitated, her gaze shifting toward the window before settling back on Harper. There was a flicker of something in her eyes—fear, perhaps, or uncertainty. "It's about Anthony—what he was working on before the attack. He was obsessed with finding something, a recipe or an ingredient, I'm not sure. But he kept saying it was the key to everything."

Harper's heart skipped a beat. She had suspected that Anthony's work was connected to the mystery surrounding the MacLeod Starter, but hearing it confirmed by someone so close to him sent a chill down her spine. "The key to what?"

"I don't know," Amelia admitted, her voice low as if she were afraid someone might overhear. "But whatever it was, it consumed him. He was always at the restaurant, staying late, poring over old books and notes. He barely slept, barely ate. I tried to get him to talk about it, but he just kept saying that he was close, that he couldn't stop now."

Harper felt a chill run down her spine. The image of Chef Anthony, once vibrant and full of life, now reduced to a shadow of himself, haunted her. She could almost see him, hunched over his work, his face gaunt with exhaustion, driven by a desperation she couldn't quite understand. "Do you think it had something to do with the MacLeod Starter?"

Amelia's eyes flickered with uncertainty. She seemed to weigh her next words carefully before responding. "It's possible. He mentioned your name a few times, said something about the starter being special, unique. But he wouldn't tell me more than that. It was like he was afraid to say too much."

Harper's mind raced with possibilities. If Chef Anthony had been onto something—something connected to her family's starter—then whoever had attacked him might still be after it. The thought made her stomach twist with fear. She had always thought of the starter as a family heirloom, a connection to her ancestors, but now it seemed like it was much more than that. It was a target.

"Thank you for telling me this," Harper said, her voice filled with sincerity. Despite the fear gnawing at her, she was grateful for Amelia's honesty. "It means a lot."

Amelia nodded, her expression serious. "Just be careful, Harper. Whatever Anthony was involved in, it's dangerous. And I have a feeling it's far from over."

As Amelia left the bakery, Harper felt a knot of anxiety tighten in her chest. The more she learned about Chef Anthony's obsession, the more she realized just how deep this mystery went. And the more she understood that the danger was growing closer with each passing day. The walls of the bakery, once a safe haven, now felt like they were closing in on her.

Harper returned to the dough she had been working on, her hands moving mechanically as her mind raced. The simple act of baking, once a source of joy and comfort, now felt like a distraction from the storm that was brewing around her. She knew she couldn't afford to be distracted—not when the stakes were so high.

The bell above the door jingled again, and Harper looked up, half-expecting to see another visitor with more unsettling news. But it was Rachel, her expression a mix of determination and concern as she hurried over to the counter.

"Harper, I've been doing some more digging," Rachel said, her voice urgent. "I think I found something."

Harper wiped her hands on a towel and motioned for Rachel to sit at one of the small tables near the window. "What is it?"

Rachel pulled out a folder from her bag, her fingers trembling slightly as she opened it and laid out a series of old documents on the table. "These are old property records, dating back to the early 1800s. I was looking for anything that might connect The Alchemists to Clover Grove, and I found something interesting."

Harper leaned in, her heart pounding as she scanned the documents. "What did you find?"

Rachel pointed to a name on one of the records, her voice barely above a whisper. "The MacLeod family owned a piece of land on the outskirts of town—land that was sold off in the late 1800s. But before it was sold, there were rumors that the land was cursed, that strange things happened there. People claimed to see lights in the woods, hear voices when no one was around."

Harper's breath caught in her throat. The idea of a cursed land, tied to her family, sent a shiver down her spine. "What happened to the land?"

"It was bought by a man named Alexander Grayson, who was known for his interest in the occult," Rachel continued. "He disappeared a few years after buying the land, and no one's heard from him since. But the land stayed in his family, passed down through the generations."

Harper felt a chill run down her spine. The pieces were starting to fit together, but the picture they were forming was one of darkness and danger. "Do you think The Alchemists are connected to this land?"

"I think it's possible," Rachel said, her voice trembling slightly. "If Alexander Grayson was involved with The Alchemists, it could explain why the land was so important. And if Chef Anthony was researching the starter, he might have stumbled onto something that led him to the land."

Harper's mind raced as she tried to process the information. The land, the starter, The Alchemists—it was all connected, but the connections were still murky, like pieces of a puzzle that hadn't yet been put together. But one thing was clear: they needed to find out what was on that land, and what connection it had to the mystery they were unraveling.

"We need to go there," Harper said, her voice filled with determination. "We need to see the land for ourselves."

Rachel nodded, though Harper could see the fear in her eyes. "We need to be careful. If The Alchemists are involved, they're not going to let us just walk in and take a look around."

"I know," Harper replied, her voice steady. "But we don't have a choice. We need to find out what Chef Anthony discovered, and why it was so important."

As they made plans to visit the land, Harper couldn't shake the feeling that they were walking into a trap. But she also knew that they couldn't back down—not now. The truth was within their reach, and they had to seize it before it slipped away.

The sun was beginning to set as Harper and Rachel left the bakery, the sky streaked with shades of orange and pink. The beauty of the evening was lost on them, their minds focused on the task ahead. The road to the land was long and winding, and as they drove, the sense of anticipation grew.

When they finally arrived, the land was bathed in the soft light of dusk. It was an eerie place, the trees tall and silent, the air heavy with the scent of damp earth. There was a stillness here, a sense of something waiting just out of sight, something ancient and powerful.

Harper and Rachel walked the perimeter of the land, their footsteps crunching on the dry leaves that littered the ground. The trees loomed overhead, their branches twisting together to form a dense canopy that blocked out the light of the setting sun.

"This place gives me the creeps," Rachel whispered, her voice barely audible.

Harper nodded, her eyes scanning the shadows for any sign of movement. "I know what you mean. But we need to keep looking. There has to be something here."

As they moved deeper into the woods, the air grew colder, the light dimmer. The trees seemed to close in around them, and Harper couldn't shake the feeling that they were being watched. Every rustle of leaves, every snap of a twig, sent her heart racing.

Finally, they came to a clearing in the woods, where the remnants of an old building stood. The structure was barely recognizable, little more than a few crumbling walls covered in moss and ivy. But there was something about it, something that sent a shiver down Harper's spine.

"This must be it," Harper said, her voice trembling slightly. "This must be where it all started."

Rachel nodded, her eyes wide with fear and awe. "What do we do now?"

Harper took a deep breath, steeling herself for what was to come. "We go inside."

KNEADING THE TRUTH

The two women approached the ruins, their footsteps echoing in the stillness. The air was thick with the scent of decay, and as they stepped inside, the temperature seemed to drop several degrees. The walls were covered in strange symbols, carved into the stone with meticulous precision.

"What is this place?" Rachel whispered, her voice filled with wonder.

Harper ran her fingers over the carvings, her heart pounding in her chest. "I don't know. But I think this is where the truth lies. This is where we'll find the answers."

As they explored the ruins, Harper couldn't shake the feeling that they were on the brink of something monumental. The secrets of the past were all around them, hidden in the stones, in the air they breathed. And as the darkness closed in, she knew that they were about to uncover the truth—a truth that would change everything.

But even as they searched, Harper couldn't ignore the sense of dread that had settled in her gut. The Alchemists were out there, watching, waiting. And she knew that they wouldn't let the secrets of the past go without a fight.

As they stood in the heart of the ruins, surrounded by the remnants of a forgotten past, Harper felt a surge of determination. She would protect the MacLeod Starter, no matter what. She would uncover the truth, and she would stop The Alchemists—whatever the cost.

But as they turned to leave, the sound of footsteps echoed through the clearing, and Harper's blood ran cold. They were not alone.

The secrets of sourdough were about to be revealed—but at what price?

Chapter 14: The Final Ingredient

The next morning, Harper woke up early, the events of the past few days weighing heavily on her mind. The sun was just beginning to rise, casting a soft golden light over the town, but the beauty of the morning did little to calm her nerves. The quiet stillness of the early hour only amplified the anxiety gnawing at her, a constant reminder that the peaceful facade of Clover Grove was about to be shattered.

As she prepared to open the bakery, Harper decided to make one last batch of sourdough using the MacLeod Starter. The process was familiar, comforting even, but there was a new sense of urgency to it—a feeling that this might be the last time she would be able to do this before everything changed. Each movement was deliberate, infused with a sense of finality that she couldn't quite shake.

She measured out the ingredients carefully, her hands steady despite the turmoil inside. Flour, water, salt, and the starter—each element coming together to create something greater than the sum of its parts. The starter, bubbling with life, seemed almost to pulse with an energy of its own, as if it too understood the gravity of the moment. As she worked, Harper thought about her ancestors, about Elspeth MacLeod and the generations of bakers who had come before her. The starter was more than just a recipe—it was a piece of history, a connection to the past, and a link to something much larger.

When the dough was ready, Harper placed it in a bowl to rise, covering it with a damp cloth. She knew that the next few hours would be crucial—that the decisions she made today could determine the future of the MacLeod Starter, and perhaps even the fate of Clover Grove. The starter had been a silent witness to centuries of history, and now it stood at the center of a conflict that had the potential to change everything.

As she waited for the dough to rise, Harper's phone buzzed with a message. It was from Ethan.

"Harper, we need to talk. I've found something. Meet me at the bakery as soon as you can."

Harper's heart skipped a beat as she read the message. She quickly replied, agreeing to meet him. Whatever Ethan had found, she knew it was important—and that it could change everything. The sense of urgency that had been simmering under the surface now boiled over, driving her to action.

When Ethan arrived at the bakery, his expression was serious, his usual easy-going demeanor replaced by a tension that mirrored Harper's own. There was a determination in his eyes that Harper hadn't seen before, a resolve that told her he understood just how high the stakes had become. He wasted no time in explaining what he had discovered.

"I did some digging into The Alchemists," Ethan said, his voice low and urgent. "They're a secret society, like Agnes said, and they've been around for centuries. Their goal is to find and control ancient knowledge—things that most people don't even believe exist. And they think the MacLeod Starter is one of those things."

Harper felt a chill run down her spine. The idea that her family's starter, something she had always thought of as a simple but cherished heirloom, could be connected to a secret society was almost too much to comprehend. "But why? What do they think it can do?"

Ethan hesitated, then said, "They believe it has the power to heal—or to harm. They think it's the key to unlocking some kind of ancient power, something that could change the world." His words hung in the air, heavy with implications that Harper was only beginning to understand.

Harper's mind raced as she processed the information. The idea that her family's starter could be connected to something so dangerous, so powerful, was both terrifying and surreal. But it also made her more determined than ever to protect it. The starter was no longer just a link to her past; it was now a crucial element in a battle she hadn't asked to be part of, but one she knew she couldn't avoid.

"What do we do now?" Harper asked, her voice steady despite the turmoil inside. The path ahead was uncertain, but she knew she couldn't afford to hesitate.

"We need to keep it safe," Ethan said, his expression serious. "Whatever The Alchemists are after, we can't let them get their hands on it. I've already put measures in place to protect you and the bakery, but we need to be vigilant. And we need to find out more about what they're planning."

Harper nodded, her resolve strengthening. The bakery, which had always been her sanctuary, now felt like the front line in a war she hadn't seen coming. "We'll figure this out, Ethan. Together."

As they stood together in the quiet bakery, Harper couldn't help but feel a deep connection to the past—a connection that was now more important than ever. The MacLeod Starter was more than just a recipe—it was a piece of history, a link to the past, and a key to the future. And Harper was determined to unlock its secrets—no matter what it took.

The morning passed in a blur of activity. Harper kept the bakery running, serving customers with a smile that felt increasingly strained as the hours ticked by. The usual rhythm of her day was punctuated by a growing sense of dread, an awareness that time was running out. Every glance at the clock, every jingle of the doorbell, felt like a countdown to an unknown but inevitable confrontation.

Rachel arrived at the bakery just before noon, her expression one of grim determination. She had spent the morning researching The Alchemists, combing through old records and texts, searching for anything that might give them an edge. Her eyes were tired, but they gleamed with the fire of discovery.

"I found something," Rachel said as she joined Harper and Ethan at the back of the bakery, where they had set up a makeshift command center of sorts. The small table was covered in books, papers, and notes, a chaotic representation of the puzzle they were trying to solve.

"What is it?" Harper asked, leaning forward with anticipation.

Rachel placed an old, leather-bound book on the table, its pages yellowed with age. "This is a journal from the late 1800s, written by a man named Alexander Grayson. He was the one who bought the land that was once owned by your family, Harper. But what's interesting is what he wrote about the land—and the starter."

Harper's breath caught in her throat. "What did he say?"

Rachel opened the journal to a marked page and began to read aloud. "Grayson wrote about a ritual, one that was meant to bind the power of the land to the MacLeod Starter. He believed that by performing this ritual, he could unlock the full potential of the starter, turning it into something far more powerful than just a tool for baking. He described it as a 'key to the divine,' something that could grant immortality or bring about destruction, depending on how it was used."

Ethan frowned, his mind clearly turning over the implications. "So, The Alchemists think that by controlling the starter, they can control this power?"

"Exactly," Rachel replied. "But there's more. Grayson wrote that the ritual required a specific ingredient, something he called 'the final ingredient.' Without it, the ritual would be incomplete, and the power would remain dormant."

Harper's heart pounded in her chest. "Do we know what the final ingredient is?"

Rachel shook her head. "Grayson never found it. He wrote that it was hidden somewhere on the land, but he didn't know where. He spent years searching for it, but he disappeared before he could find it."

A heavy silence settled over the room as they all absorbed the implications. The final ingredient—the missing piece of the puzzle—was still out there, waiting to be discovered. And if The Alchemists found it first, the consequences could be catastrophic.

"We need to find it," Ethan said, his voice resolute. "Before they do."

Harper nodded, her mind already racing with possibilities. "We need to go back to the land. We need to search every inch of it until we find that ingredient."

Rachel hesitated, a flicker of fear crossing her face. "Harper, that land is dangerous. We don't know what's out there—or who might be watching."

"I know," Harper replied, her voice firm. "But we don't have a choice. We can't let The Alchemists complete the ritual. If they do, everything we've been trying to protect could be lost."

Ethan placed a reassuring hand on Harper's shoulder. "We'll go together. We'll be careful. But we need to move quickly. Every moment we wait gives them a chance to get ahead of us."

The resolve in Ethan's eyes gave Harper the strength she needed. She knew the risks, understood the danger, but she also knew that she couldn't back down. The starter, the land, the final ingredient—they were all pieces of a puzzle that had to be solved. And she was the one who had to solve it.

They made plans to return to the land that evening, when the cover of darkness would give them a better chance of avoiding detection. The hours leading up to their departure were tense, filled with last-minute preparations and a growing sense of urgency. Harper and Rachel gathered supplies—flashlights, maps, notebooks—while Ethan checked and double-checked the security measures he had put in place at the bakery.

As the sun dipped below the horizon, casting long shadows over the town, Harper felt a sense of finality settle over her. This was it. The moment they had been building toward. Whatever happened tonight would determine the course of everything that followed.

They arrived at the land just as the last light of day faded into night. The woods were eerily quiet, the trees casting dark, twisted shadows across the ground. The air was thick with the scent of earth and decay, a reminder that this place had been abandoned for a reason.

Armed with flashlights, they began their search, moving methodically through the trees, their footsteps muffled by the thick layer of leaves and undergrowth. The woods felt alive, every rustle of leaves, every creak of branches sending a shiver down Harper's spine. She couldn't shake the feeling that they were being watched, that something—or someone—was lurking just out of sight.

They reached the clearing where the old ruins stood, the remnants of the building now nothing more than crumbling stone walls covered in moss and ivy. The symbols etched into the stone seemed to glow in the moonlight, their meaning just out of reach.

"This is where we start," Harper said, her voice barely above a whisper. She could feel the weight of the past pressing down on her, the sense that they were standing at the threshold of something ancient and powerful.

They split up, each taking a section of the ruins to search for any clue, any sign of the final ingredient. Harper moved slowly, her flashlight beam cutting through the darkness as she examined the stones, her fingers tracing the symbols carved into the walls. The air was thick with anticipation, every sound amplified in the silence.

Minutes turned into hours as they searched, the tension growing with each passing moment. Harper's mind raced, the pieces of the puzzle swirling around in her head, but the final piece—the one that would make everything clear—remained elusive.

Just as Harper was beginning to lose hope, Rachel called out from across the clearing. "Harper! Ethan! I think I found something!"

Harper's heart leaped in her chest as she rushed over to where Rachel was standing, Ethan close behind. Rachel was kneeling beside a section of the wall that had partially collapsed, her flashlight illuminating something buried beneath the rubble.

"It's a box," Rachel said, her voice filled with excitement. She carefully cleared away the debris, revealing a small, ornately carved wooden box. The wood was dark and polished, the carvings intricate and detailed, depicting scenes of nature—trees, rivers, mountains. The craftsmanship was exquisite, the box clearly ancient, yet remarkably well-preserved.

Harper's hands trembled as she reached for the box, her fingers brushing against the cool wood. There was a sense of reverence in the air, as if they were in the presence of something sacred.

"Do you think this is it?" Ethan asked, his voice hushed.

Harper nodded, her heart pounding in her chest. "It has to be. This must be the final ingredient."

She carefully lifted the lid of the box, revealing a small, glass vial filled with a shimmering liquid. The liquid seemed to glow in the darkness, its light pulsing with an otherworldly energy. Harper could feel the power emanating from it, a force that was both awe-inspiring and terrifying.

"This is it," Harper whispered, her voice filled with a mixture of awe and fear. "This is what they were looking for."

As she held the vial in her hands, Harper felt the weight of the responsibility that had been passed down to her. The power of the MacLeod Starter, the final ingredient, the legacy of her ancestors—it was all connected, all part of a larger plan that she was only beginning to understand.

But even as she marveled at the discovery, Harper knew that their journey was far from over. They had found the final ingredient, but now they had to protect it—because The Alchemists would stop at nothing to get their hands on it.

As they made their way back through the woods, Harper couldn't shake the feeling that they were being followed. Every rustle of leaves, every snap of a twig, sent a jolt of fear through her. The darkness seemed to press in on them, the trees closing ranks as if trying to trap them.

But they pressed on, driven by the knowledge that they were now the keepers of something extraordinary, something that could change the world.

When they finally reached the safety of the car, Harper let out a breath she hadn't realized she was holding. They had done it. They had found the final ingredient. But as they drove away from the land, the vial safely tucked away in Harper's bag, she knew that the real battle was just beginning.

The Alchemists would come for them—of that, she was certain. And when they did, Harper would be ready. The final ingredient, the MacLeod Starter, the legacy of her family—it was all in her hands now.

And she would protect it, no matter what.

Recipe: MacLeod Family Sourdough Brownies
Ingredients:

- 1/2 cup sourdough discard
- 1/2 cup butter, melted
- 1 cup sugar
- 1/2 cup cocoa powder
- 1/2 teaspoon vanilla extract
- 2 eggs
- 1/2 cup all-purpose flour
- 1/4 teaspoon salt
- 1/2 teaspoon baking powder

Instructions:

1. Preheat your oven to 350°F (175°C). Grease an 8x8-inch baking pan or line it with parchment paper.
2. In a large mixing bowl, combine the melted butter, sugar, and cocoa powder. Stir until well combined.
3. Add the eggs, one at a time, mixing well after each addition. Stir in the vanilla extract.
4. Add the sourdough discard and mix until fully incorporated.
5. In a separate bowl, whisk together the flour, salt, and baking powder. Gradually add the dry ingredients to the wet ingredients, stirring until just combined.
6. Pour the batter into the prepared baking pan and spread it out evenly.
7. Bake for 25-30 minutes, or until a toothpick inserted into the center comes out with just a few moist crumbs.
8. Allow the brownies to cool completely in the pan before cutting them into squares.

Enjoy these rich, fudgy sourdough brownies as a treat with a cup of coffee or tea!

Chapter 15: The Gathering Storm

The discovery of the final ingredient marked a turning point in the battle Harper and her friends were waging against The Alchemists. The vial, with its shimmering liquid, was a powerful artifact, but it was also a magnet for danger. Harper knew that from the moment they had unearthed it, their lives had irrevocably changed. The small, quiet town of Clover Grove was no longer just a backdrop for their lives; it was now the stage for a conflict that had been brewing for centuries.

The day after their discovery, Harper, Rachel, and Ethan gathered in the bakery, their faces etched with concern. The vial sat in the center of the table, its glow muted in the daylight but still pulsing with a quiet, insistent energy. It seemed to draw their gazes, as if it were a living thing demanding their attention.

"We need to figure out our next move," Ethan said, breaking the silence. His voice was steady, but Harper could sense the undercurrent of tension in it. "The Alchemists will come for this, and we need to be ready."

Harper nodded, her mind racing. "We need to understand what this liquid is, what it can do, and how it connects to the starter. If The Alchemists want it so badly, there must be a reason."

Rachel, who had been quietly examining the vial, looked up. "I've been thinking about that. This vial—it might be more than just an ingredient. It could be a catalyst, something that amplifies the power of the starter. If that's the case, The

Alchemists might be trying to use it to perform some kind of ritual, one that could give them control over the power they've been seeking."

"That makes sense," Harper said, her thoughts aligning with Rachel's. "But if we're right, then that means we have an even bigger problem. If they complete the ritual, they could unleash something we don't fully understand—something that could be catastrophic."

Ethan leaned forward, his expression grim. "We can't let that happen. We need to stay one step ahead of them. Harper, is there anything in your family's records, anything at all, that might give us a clue about how to counter this?"

Harper bit her lip, her mind sifting through the countless journals and letters she had read. "There are references to rituals, but nothing specific about this kind of power. Most of the records focus on the starter as a tool for healing, for nourishment. But there is one thing..."

Rachel and Ethan both looked at her expectantly.

"My grandmother once mentioned a legend, something about a guardian of the starter. It was a story passed down through generations, but she always said it was just a myth. The guardian was supposed to be someone who could wield the power of the starter, someone who could protect it from those who would use it for harm."

"Do you think it's true?" Ethan asked, his eyes narrowing with interest.

"I don't know," Harper admitted. "But if there's any truth to it, then maybe the guardian isn't just a myth. Maybe it's someone real, someone who's supposed to protect the starter—and this vial."

Rachel frowned. "But who could it be? And if there is a guardian, why haven't they shown up yet?"

Harper shook her head, frustration bubbling up inside her. "I don't know. But we need to find out. We need to dig deeper, look into every record, every story. There has to be something we've missed."

Ethan nodded, his expression resolute. "Then we do that. We go through everything, piece by piece. We're not letting The Alchemists win this."

The next few days were a blur of research and planning. Harper, Rachel, and Ethan spent hours poring over old texts, searching for any mention of the guardian, the vial, or the ritual that The Alchemists might be trying to perform. The bakery became their headquarters, the table in the back room covered in books and papers, the air thick with the scent of coffee and determination.

Harper barely slept, her mind too full of possibilities, her body running on adrenaline and the occasional cup of strong coffee. She felt the weight of the responsibility pressing down on her, the knowledge that the fate of the starter—and perhaps even more—rested in her hands. But she also felt a strange sense of clarity, a focus that drove her forward despite the exhaustion.

Finally, after days of searching, they found something—a reference in one of the oldest journals, a single sentence that seemed to hold the key to everything they had been trying to understand.

"The guardian will rise when the final ingredient is found, and the power of the earth and sky will be theirs to command."

Harper read the sentence aloud, her voice barely above a whisper. The words seemed to hang in the air, heavy with meaning.

"That's it," Rachel said, her eyes wide. "The guardian isn't just a myth. It's real. And whoever it is, they're connected to the final ingredient. They're supposed to wield the power—but only when the ingredient is found."

Ethan looked at Harper, his expression serious. "Do you think it could be you, Harper? Could you be the guardian?"

Harper's heart skipped a beat at the suggestion. The idea was both exhilarating and terrifying. She had always felt a connection to the starter, a deep, almost instinctual understanding of its power. But to be the guardian? To be the one who was meant to protect it, to wield its power?

"I don't know," she said, her voice trembling slightly. "But if I am, then we need to figure out what that means—and fast."

Rachel nodded, her mind already racing ahead. "We need to find out how to awaken the guardian's power, how to use the final ingredient. If you are the guardian, Harper, then you're our best chance at stopping The Alchemists."

Ethan placed a hand on Harper's shoulder, his touch grounding her in the moment. "We're with you, Harper. Whatever happens, we'll face it together."

The words gave Harper the strength she needed. She knew that the road ahead would be difficult, that the stakes were higher than she had ever imagined. But she also knew that she wasn't alone. With Rachel and Ethan by her side, she felt ready to face whatever was coming.

And she knew that whatever happened, she would do everything in her power to protect the starter, the final ingredient, and the legacy of her family.

Chapter 16: The Ritual Begins

The day of the confrontation with The Alchemists dawned with a sense of foreboding that settled over Clover Grove like a thick fog. The sun struggled to break through the clouds, casting the town in a dim, eerie light. It felt as if the world itself was holding its breath, waiting for the storm to break.

Harper, Rachel, and Ethan gathered in the bakery, the final preparations underway. The vial, now securely hidden, was at the center of their plans, but it also represented their greatest vulnerability. If The Alchemists found it before they were ready, everything they had worked for would be lost.

"We need to draw them out," Ethan said, his voice tense. "We can't just wait for them to come to us. We need to make the first move, take the fight to them."

"But how?" Rachel asked, her brow furrowed with concern. "We don't even know where they are."

Harper's mind raced, the pieces of the puzzle coming together in a way that felt almost inevitable. "The land," she said suddenly, her voice filled with certainty. "We found the final ingredient there. That's where they'll try to complete the ritual. If we go back, we can intercept them, stop them before they can do anything."

Ethan nodded, his expression hardening with resolve. "Then that's what we'll do. We go back to the land, and we stop them—whatever it takes."

The plan was risky, but they all knew it was their only option. They gathered their supplies, every movement tinged with urgency. As they prepared to leave, Harper took one last look around the bakery, her heart heavy with the knowledge that she might not return. The bakery had been her sanctuary, the place where she had found peace and purpose. Now, it was the starting point of a journey that could end in triumph or disaster.

They arrived at the land as the sun dipped below the horizon, casting long shadows across the ground. The air was thick with tension, the silence oppressive. The ruins stood as a stark reminder of the past, a symbol of the power that had been sought and lost over the centuries.

Harper felt the weight of history pressing down on her, the knowledge that she was standing on the threshold of something monumental. The ground beneath her feet seemed to hum with energy, the final ingredient in her bag pulsing with a power that felt both familiar and foreign.

They moved cautiously through the trees, their senses heightened, every sound amplified in the stillness. The air was cool, carrying with it the scent of earth and decay, a reminder that this place had seen more than its share of death.

As they reached the clearing where the ruins stood, they saw them—The Alchemists. A group of figures, cloaked in shadow, stood around a stone altar that had been erected in the center of the clearing. The air crackled with energy, the symbols on the stone glowing faintly in the dim light.

Harper's heart pounded in her chest as she realized the full extent of the danger they were facing. The Alchemists were here, and they were ready to perform the ritual.

"We have to stop them," Harper whispered, her voice trembling with fear and determination.

Ethan nodded, his jaw clenched. "We can't let them finish."

They moved quickly, but as they stepped into the clearing, the leader of The Alchemists turned to face them. His eyes were cold, calculating, and filled with a dark intelligence that sent a shiver down Harper's spine.

"You're too late," he said, his voice dripping with malice. "The ritual has already begun."

Harper's heart sank as she realized the truth. The symbols on the altar were glowing brighter now, the energy in the air growing more intense. The ground beneath their feet seemed to vibrate with a power that was building, reaching a crescendo.

"No!" Harper cried, stepping forward, her hands clenched into fists. "I won't let you do this!"

The leader of The Alchemists smiled, a cold, cruel smile. "You can't stop what's already in motion, girl. The power of the earth and sky will be ours."

But Harper wasn't willing to give up. She could feel the final ingredient in her bag, the vial pulsing with energy, calling to her. She knew, with a certainty that went beyond reason, that she had to act—now.

In one swift motion, Harper pulled the vial from her bag and held it high, the liquid inside glowing with an otherworldly light. The leader's eyes widened in shock as he realized what she was holding.

"No!" he shouted, lunging toward her, but it was too late.

Harper smashed the vial against the stone altar, the liquid spilling out and seeping into the cracks of the stone. The air around them exploded with energy, a blinding light engulfing the clearing, the power of the earth and sky converging in a single, brilliant flash.

KNEADING THE TRUTH

For a moment, everything was silent. The world seemed to hold its breath, suspended in a state of perfect stillness. And then, with a sound like thunder, the energy was released, surging through the ruins, the trees, the very ground itself.

The force of it knocked Harper off her feet, sending her sprawling onto the ground. She felt the energy pass through her, filling her with a warmth that was both comforting and terrifying. It was as if the power of the earth and sky had entered her, fusing with her very being.

When the light finally faded, Harper slowly sat up, her body trembling with the aftershocks of the energy that had coursed through her. The clearing was silent, the ruins bathed in the soft glow of moonlight. The Alchemists were gone, their presence erased by the power of the ritual.

Ethan and Rachel rushed to her side, their faces etched with concern. "Harper, are you okay?" Rachel asked, her voice filled with worry.

Harper nodded, though she could still feel the lingering effects of the energy inside her. "I'm okay," she said, her voice hoarse. "But...I think something's changed."

Ethan helped her to her feet, his gaze searching her face for any sign of injury. "What do you mean?"

Harper took a deep breath, trying to make sense of the sensations swirling inside her. "I think...I think I'm the guardian. The ritual—when I broke the vial, it did something. I can feel the power inside me, the power of the starter, the earth, everything. It's like...it's like I'm connected to it now."

Rachel stared at her, awe in her eyes. "Harper, that's incredible. But what does it mean? What do we do now?"

Harper looked around the clearing, the remnants of the altar still glowing faintly in the moonlight. She knew, deep in her soul, that the battle wasn't over. The Alchemists might have been defeated, but the power they sought was still out there—inside her.

"We go home," Harper said finally, her voice steady. "We figure out what this means, what I'm supposed to do. The starter, the final ingredient—it's all part of something bigger, something I need to understand."

As they left the clearing and made their way back through the woods, Harper felt a new sense of purpose settle over her. She was the guardian now, the protector of a power that had been sought for centuries. And she knew that her journey was far from over.

The final ingredient had been found, the ritual stopped—but the legacy of the MacLeod family was only just beginning to unfold. And Harper was ready to face whatever came next, no matter what it took.

Chapter 17: The Dawn of a New Legacy

The days following the confrontation with The Alchemists were a whirlwind of recovery and reflection. Harper, Rachel, and Ethan returned to Clover Grove, their bodies and minds weary from the battle they had fought. But the town, with its quiet streets and familiar faces, offered them a brief respite, a chance to catch their breath before they figured out what came next.

The bakery, once a symbol of routine and comfort, now felt different to Harper. Every time she stepped inside, she felt the power of the starter thrumming beneath the surface, a constant reminder of the responsibility she now carried. The air was thick with a sense of potential, as if the very walls of the bakery were charged with the energy of the final ingredient, the guardian, and the legacy of her family.

Harper knew that she couldn't go back to the way things were. The discovery of the final ingredient, the confrontation with The Alchemists, and the realization that she was the guardian had changed everything. She was no longer just a baker, no longer just the keeper of an ancient starter. She was now the protector of something far greater, something that could shape the future in ways she was only beginning to comprehend.

As she worked in the bakery, Harper found herself drawn to the starter, spending hours tending to it, feeling its energy pulse through her hands as she kneaded dough, its life force now deeply intertwined with her own. It was as if the starter was trying to communicate with her, to guide her toward something important—something she needed to understand.

Rachel and Ethan continued to support her, their friendship now cemented by the trials they had faced together. Rachel threw herself into research, determined to help Harper make sense of her new role, while Ethan focused on ensuring the safety of the bakery and the town. The bond between them had grown stronger, forged in the heat of battle and tempered by the knowledge that they were all part of something much larger.

One morning, as Harper prepared to open the bakery, she felt a strange sense of calm wash over her. The sun was just beginning to rise, casting a soft golden light over the town, and the air was crisp and cool. It was the kind of morning that promised a new beginning, a fresh start.

As she worked, Harper found herself thinking about her grandmother, about the stories she had told her as a child, stories of the MacLeod family and their connection to the land, to the earth, to the power of the starter. She realized now that those stories had been more than just tales—they had been a way of preparing her for the role she was destined to play.

The guardian was not just a protector of the starter; she was a bridge between the past and the future, a keeper of knowledge that had been passed down through generations. Harper understood now that her journey was not just about stopping The Alchemists—it was about embracing her heritage, understanding the power she had been entrusted with, and using it to guide the world toward a better future.

As the day went on, Harper's sense of purpose grew stronger. She knew that the time had come to fully accept her role as the guardian, to step into the legacy that had been waiting for her. And she knew that she couldn't do it alone.

That evening, as the sun set over Clover Grove, Harper gathered Rachel and Ethan in the bakery. They sat around the small table in the back room, the same table where they had planned their confrontation with The Alchemists, but now the atmosphere was different. There was a sense of hope, of possibility, that hadn't been there before.

"I've been thinking a lot about what comes next," Harper began, her voice steady. "I know that I'm the guardian, and I know that I have a responsibility to protect the starter and the power it holds. But I also know that I can't do this alone. I need your help—both of you."

Rachel and Ethan exchanged a glance before nodding in unison. "We're with you, Harper," Rachel said, her voice filled with determination. "Whatever you need, we'll be there."

Ethan leaned forward, his expression serious. "We've come this far together, Harper. We're not going to let you face this alone."

Harper felt a surge of gratitude for her friends, for the bond they had forged. "Thank you," she said, her voice thick with emotion. "I couldn't ask for better allies."

As they discussed their plans for the future, Harper felt a sense of excitement building inside her. She knew that there would be challenges ahead, that The Alchemists might not be gone for good, but she also knew that they had the strength and the knowledge to face whatever came their way.

The power of the starter, the legacy of the MacLeod family, the role of the guardian—it was all part of a new beginning, a new chapter in the story of Clover Grove. And Harper was ready to embrace it, to step into the role she had been born to play.

As the night wore on, the bakery was filled with the sound of laughter and the smell of freshly baked bread. The future was uncertain, but for the first time in a long time, Harper felt at peace. She knew that she was exactly where she was meant to be, surrounded by the people she loved, ready to face whatever came next.

And as the moon rose high in the sky, casting a silver light over the town, Harper knew that the dawn of a new legacy had begun.

Don't miss out!

Visit the website below and you can sign up to receive emails whenever Gracelynne MacAllister publishes a new book. There's no charge and no obligation.

https://books2read.com/r/B-A-CCFLC-FLJZE

BOOKS 2 READ

Connecting independent readers to independent writers.

www.ingramcontent.com/pod-product-compliance
Lightning Source LLC
LaVergne TN
LVHW041549050325
805180LV00006B/78